THE DEA

THE DEATH TRAIL

by

M. Duggan

Dales Large Print Books
Long Preston, North Yorkshire,
BD23 4ND, England.

British Library Cataloguing in Publication Data.

Duggan, M.
  The death trail.

  A catalogue record of this book is
  available from the British Library

  ISBN   978-1-84262-683-2 pbk

First published in Great Britain 2008 by Robert Hale Ltd.

Copyright © M. Duggan 2008

Cover illustration © Gordon Crabb courtesy of Alison Eldred

The right of M. Duggan to be identified as the author of this work has been asserted by him in accordance with the Copyright, Designs and Patents Act, 1988

Published in Large Print 2009 by arrangement with Robert Hale Ltd.

Dales Large Print is an imprint of Library Magna Books Ltd.

Printed and bound in Great Britain by
T.J. (International) Ltd., Cornwall, PL28 8RW

CHAPTER 1

Tending bar was damned hard work. A man needed eyes on the side of his head if the trouble that inevitably threatened to erupt was to be averted. He was good at his job, and good averting trouble. The regular patrons of this place on the wrong side of town knew better than to cross Noah Swan. The bartender was a permanent fixture. He knew by name or sight the majority of the riffraff who chose to patronize Flannigan's Bar.

When the woman staggered in from the street he recognized her. Most folk called her Red Polly because of her bright-red hair. And maybe because of her brightly rouged cheeks. He watched as she staggered to a corner table, sat down and then promptly passed out, head resting on her arms. It wouldn't surprise him if one day she were found dead in the gutter. She was on the road to destruction, a dangerous woman by all accounts, one who would destroy herself. He would let her sleep off the effects of the cheap booze she had been guzzling. When dawn broke she could stagger back to wherever it was she holed up for the day.

The orders came quickly and he kept pouring the drinks. The old potman Flannigan employed was rushed off his feet. When trouble erupted the potman was no goddamn use but as long as there was a plentiful supply of clean glasses Noah didn't give a damn. He didn't need anyone fighting his corner.

The five young men who had just strolled in had his attention. They did not belong here. Their fine clothes set them apart. Their kind drifted in from time to time bored and looking for excitement, seeking a taste of dangerous living.

Throughout the evening he continued to watch them without seeming to do so. And he noticed that they were showing particular interest in the insensible Polly. When two of them taking her beneath the arms stood her up and began to steer her towards the door they really did get his attention. He knew instinctively they were up to no good. Their intentions towards the insensible woman were real bad.

'You must leave her here, gentlemen.' Noah forced himself to smile. He wanted to defuse the situation. In the case of a fracas the law inevitably sided with the rich and privileged.

'What the hell do you mean, telling your betters what to do?' The leader of this pack of dogs turned his attention to Noah. He was a tall, good-looking young man, the kind of young man ladies of a certain age might want to favour, Noah thought, as he held the other man's gaze. 'You need a lesson in manners, bartender. You need to know when to keep your long nose out of matters that are not your concern. One day, someone is going to slice off that nose!'

The threat hung between them. A lesser man might have told them just to get and watched them take the woman with them, but not Noah. He never backed down.

'Leave the woman,' he ordered flatly.

They dropped Polly and she fell to the floor, an inelegant sight with a rumpled skirt, grimy petticoat and a great deal of exposed leg. But she remained oblivious to everything.

Men began to move away from Noah and the five young gentlemen. He had come out from behind the bar now; his shotgun pointing downwards, it was true, but he was ready for action.

The handsome young man gave a sneering

smile. 'I am Nathaniel Standish. If you pull that trigger, bartender, you will be sure to hang. Perhaps you have heard of my father, Judge Elmore Standish?'

Noah had indeed heard of the judge. The judge called the shots in this city. And indeed if he were to shoot one of these fine young gentlemen he would be looking at years behind bars. And a rope if he were to kill one of them!

He wanted this over with quickly. It wasn't his way to exchange meaningless words. There was only one way to deal with this drunken bunch, and they *were* drunk, he could see that. So, not giving them time to collect their thoughts, he went on the attack. He dropped his shotgun and grasped the fancy shirt of the man who'd elected himself leader. He jerked the young fool towards him, brought his own head forward and struck the other man's forehead with a rc-sounding thud. He'd pulled this trick before and it always worked. The fine young gentleman fell to the sawdust and Noah could not help but deliver a kick for good measure. He'd been challenged, after all, and in this bar his word was law.

He pulled the cudgel he always carried from his belt and used it to good effect, swinging it with deadly precision. Banged heads and vicious jabs to stomachs quickly knocked the stuffing out of them. Their reactions had been slowed by drink, and even sober they would have been no match for him. He had been obliged to do this many times before. This was nothing new. Here fracas was normal.

'Get them out of my bar,' he ordered. 'Dump them in the gutter where they belong.' To his surprise none of his patrons made a move to carry out his instructions but no matter, as the group were lurching out, two of them supporting a semiconscious Nathaniel Standish.

'His pa is Judge Standish,' one of them croaked before they got themselves out of the bar.

'Yep, and my pa is making merry with the devil!' Noah rejoined. 'Settle down, folks. Potman, sweep up the broken glasses!' Stooping he hauled Polly, who was a considerable weight, behind the bar. When she came round she could stagger out under her own steam.

'She ain't worth it, Noah. She ain't worth it,' the potman advised. 'You've brought big trouble upon yourself. You wait and see. You ain't heard the last of this. No one in his right mind messes with the judge and his boy!'

Noah shrugged. He had work to do. The orders were coming in fast and furious. He noted that some of the customers were voicing their agreement with the potman. But what the hell! A man could not spend his life worrying about what might happen, at least not a man such as himself.

When the last of the customers had staggered out into the grey dawn of day and the potman had disappeared into a backroom, collapsing upon a mattress oblivious to all until the evening shift started, Noah brewed coffee. The bar was closed now for an hour or so until the day workers arrived. All Noah had to do was mop up, sprinkle fresh sawdust, and wipe over the tables and then he would be done.

A young galoot slumped at a corner table got his attention. At first he thought the man was drunk. He generally sobered them up with a coffee. This time a closer inspection showed that something was wrong. Cautiously he touched flesh that should have been warm but found only coldness. There was no pulse.

Damn. He'd died here and Noah hadn't noticed until now. There was no sign of injury; violence seemingly had not occasioned this particular death. Without giving it much thought he went through the corpse's pockets, looking for identification. As the man had died in his bar he guessed it fell to him to write to any kin. He browsed through the bundle of letters found in an inside pocket.

'Hell! If that don't beat all!' he exclaimed softly. For the first time in a long time he was surprised.

'Get the hell out of here, Noah,' a voice belonging to Flannigan, owner of the bar and Noah's employer, exclaimed loudly. 'You're fired. It's for your own good. Elmore Standish'll have you beaten to a pulp. He is rounding up his bully boys as we speak.' Flannigan paused. 'Get the hell out of here, Noah, for my sake if not your own. If they find you here they'll smash my livelihood to smithereens. They may even smash me to smithereens for good measure. Please, Noah, I'm begging you! Leave town! There's not an employer in the city will hire you now. Standish has put the word out. You've been marked, Noah, marked!'

Noah didn't reply. He put on his jacket, stuffed the bundle of correspondence taken from the dead customer into an inside pocket and disappeared into the rain that had begun to fall outside.

'What the hell!' a voice croaked. Miz Polly, using the bar for support, hauled herself upright.

'Get the hell out of my bar. You no account floozie!' Flannigan bellowed. 'Nathaniel Standish has laid a charge of theft against you. Seems you took his watch. Seems they'll find it on you when they take you in. That's the only interest they had in you, getting back the watch you lifted.'

She didn't know what the hell Flannigan was yapping about. She searched her pockets and did not find a watch. But god-damnit she could not remember whether she had lifted the watch or not. Her stomach heaved but she managed to keep down the little food she had eaten.

An inner voice which she generally ignored now warned her to get out of town. She shoved Flannigan out of the way. She paused to stop beside the galoot who was clearly dead. Without compunction she rifled his pockets and quickly pocketed the money she found.

Flannigan thought to remonstrate, then decided against it. This woman had a reputation and a violent one at that. He felt suddenly weary. All he wanted was for her to get

14

out his bar. He had lost a good man because of her!

'I've fired the bum,' Flannigan declared as the judge's men burst into the bar. 'I've told him any man who turns on his betters ain't wanted in my place. And I've kicked that drunken whore out. I guess she's crawled into a doorway, holed up until the rain stops. As for Noah Swan, well, I reckon he's headed for his rooming house.'

Judge Elmore Standish walked into the bar. 'Be very careful what you say about my son,' he warned Flannigan softly. 'Now tell me! Where does he room?'

Without hesitation Flannigan supplied the information. If Noah Swan had been fool enough to return to his rooming house he deserved to get what was coming his way.

'Go find him,' Standish ordered the hirelings. 'And see that you break every bone in his body.'

Noah Swan headed for the railway station. His stomach growled. He needed to eat. At any moment he expected to be stopped, to be forced to fight for his life, but nothing happened except that rain continued to fall with gusto.

15

Miz Polly also headed for the station. Mud splashed up by carriages splattered her tawdry gown. Already she was soaked to the skin. She stumbled into the station ignoring the looks of disgust directed her way by respectable women, who hurriedly stepped out of her path.

'Give me a ticket.' She glared at the clerk. 'Say, don't I know you? Didn't we...'

'Take your ticket,' the clerk interrupted hurriedly. 'It'll take you as far as you want to go.'

Noah Swan settled back against the upholstery. He was a city man. He'd been born and raised in this city. And now he was headed for some goddamn frontier town known as Hawk's Head. Events had moved fast. His life had been turned upside down. He'd been unsettled. There'd be no bar to tend tonight. No customers to tend. No conversations to listen to, no fools to save from themselves, no dangerous customers to be kept in line.

The whistle hooted and the train began to move. He felt himself relax. A door was pulled open and a figure tumbled into the carriage. Miz Polly stumbled to a window seat and sank back against the upholstery. She glared at him and he glared right back. He wasn't fool enough to expect any thanks

16

for saving Miz Polly's worthless hide.

'You cause any trouble on this train, Miz Polly, and I'll throw you out of the door!'

'You come anywhere near me, Mr Noah, and I'll gut you like a fish,' she rejoined unabashed. She continued to regard him with baleful eyes, then, clenching her jaw she turned her head away and stared resolutely from the window.

Which suited him just fine. The woman was poison. But he had done what was right last night. He did not regret it.

Beyond the windows of the train the rain continued to fall.

The man whose place he was now taking had been an exemplary man by the sound of it, a far better man than Noah Swan, whose only ambition was to own his own establishment. But this man, this Mr Noah, whose place he was taking, had been a schoolteacher.

Noah Swan didn't give a damn about young minds. He was on his way to Hawk's Head simply because the late Mr Noah, the deceased schoolteacher, had purchased a ticket for Hawk's Head. Noah reasoned that there was sure to be a saloon in Hawk's Head, maybe two or three, and being a damn good barkeeper he was sure he would land on his feet.

It was true that he had never envisaged himself working in a frontier town. He was a city man. But he knew that he could handle anything the customers of the Hawk's Head saloons might throw at him. His job was to serve the drinks and stop the fancy mirrors from being smashed to pieces. He guessed it wasn't that important where the establishment was situated.

Miz Polly spotted the conductor approaching, a short-legged pot-bellied little galoot. For his sake he had better not be looking for trouble!

Noah hoped the man wouldn't be fool enough to rile her. Miz Polly, he was sure, was capable of gutting the luckless conductor like a fish. True, she was sober now, but her temperament sober or drunk was vicious.

'Ma'am,' the conductor said, 'I have something here that you left in my box car. It's your valise, ma'am. You'll need to change into something more comfortable.'

She merely glared at him.

He opened the valise. 'It was left behind,' he whispered. 'What you have on looks mighty chilly. I reckon you'll find something to suit.'

Polly took the valise. 'I reckon,' she agreed.

Tubbs, the conductor, nodded. She headed for the box car to put on respectable clothing. And then he spotted the hard-eyed *hombre*, clean-shaven with closely cropped hair, watching him.

'Don't you even think of pestering that woman,' the conductor warned softly. 'I'll not countenance unseemly behaviour on my train.'

Noah bit back an angry report. He'd been ready to save the damn fool's hide if needs be. And as for pestering Polly who, he suspected, had dispatched at least one of her clients, well that was the last thing on his mind.

'Nonsense, conductor,' a female voice rebuked him sharply. 'You are speaking to a respectable man, a gentleman.'

'Well, in that case I apologize, sir,' Tubbs replied smoothly, not wanting to tangle with the irate spinster who had unexpectedly decided to defend a man who, Tubbs suspected, was no gentleman.

'Forgive my presumption, sir.' She sat down beside Noah. 'But I could not allow that vile assumption to remain unchallenged. I am Miss Agatha Webb, sister of Pastor Webb of Hawk's Head.'

'I'm called Noah,' he reluctantly replied.

19

He wanted to get rid of her. He had no intention of striking up an acquaintance with a pastor's sister who doubtless, when she discovered his profession was that of barkeeper, would be suitably shocked.

'Disreputable women ought not to be allowed to travel alongside respectable women! What do you think, Mr Noah?'

Noah stifled a groan It was going to be a long journey.

Theodore Black sighed with pretended regret. 'You've admitted it. You took my steer.'

'It had a broken leg, Mr Black. It was almost dead. I just put the critter out of its misery.' The dirt farmer was shaking with fear.

'You'll have a few good feasts out of my steer! Ain't that so?' the rancher continued remorselessly. The luckless farmer did not reply.

'Answer Mr Black, damnit!' Black's ramrod punched the man in the mouth breaking teeth and splattering blood. The man's wife, who was being restrained by two of Black's men, began to scream. Three small girls clung to her skins. Two boys had been hogtied to stop them trying to interfere with the proceedings.

'The evidence is there for all to see.' The

rancher indicated the remains of the butchered steer. 'This ain't no lynching. I have two members of the town council here as witnesses that an innocent man has not been railroaded. Dobbs here is guilty. If anyone thinks different speak up.'

No one spoke except the man's wife who sobbed for mercy.

'When will you farming folk understand?' Black continued patiently. 'If I let one of you get away with taking a steer there are a dozen more of you just waiting to help yourselves. All of you saying you'd just put a critter out of its miser. Well, I'm going to have to make an example of you, Dobbs!' Black paused for good effect before roaring, 'String him up!'

Dobbs, not being man enough to die decently, began to cry and beg for mercy. Black regarded the snivelling varmint with distaste, watching expressionlessly as the hanging rope soared over the tree branch. Dobbs went berserk as his arms were tied behind him. They couldn't get him on to a horse because of his threshing legs, so they made do with an old wooden crate. Threshing legs were secured, the crate was kicked away as the noose went around his neck.

Dobbs took a long time to die. Some of the

hard-bitten crew looked away as the dirt farmer rope-danced and choked to death whilst others rolled themselves smokes. Theodore Black lit a fancy cigar. He didn't speak until the hanging was over. 'Where the hell is my boy? Where the hell is Freddy?'

'I can't say, boss,' the ramrod answered respectfully. 'Shall we bury the varmint?'

'Yep, get digging. Mrs Dobbs ain't in a state to bury him in her condition.' Black prided himself on being a fair man. 'I ain't burning your shack, ma'am, given your condition. Now Dobbs was a no-account varmint. You find yourself a decent man. Forget about Dobbs.'

'You'll burn in hell for this, Theodore Black,' the woman screamed hysterically. 'And get your bloodstained hands off my man. I'll bury him myself.'

'As you wish, ma'am,' the rancher replied absentmindedly. Where the hell was his son, young Freddy?

'Say!' the ramrod exclaimed 'Ain't it today the train is due to arrive? I'd guess Freddy has gone into town to meet the train. The new schoolteacher is due to arrive on that train, ain't he?' The man chuckled, 'School-teachers and young Freddy don't get along!'

'So that young varmint has sneaked into

town whilst I have been otherwise occu-pied.' Theodore Black laughed. There was a note of pride in his voice. 'That's my boy!' He looked at his watch. 'Boys, we had best get to town and save the schoolteacher's hide!' He shook his head but those around him could see he was amused rather than displeased.

CHAPTER 2

By the time they reached Hawk's Head Polly was wishing she hadn't got on the goddamn train. She was a city woman. She didn't belong in a frontier town. How the hell, she wondered, was she going to survive?

Noah was tired of the twittering Miss Agatha who, he had discovered, read her Bible every morning without fail. He stepped down on to the platform, and wished he had never got on the goddamn train. He took a deep breath. The smell here was different from the smell of the narrow streets he was used to.

'Goddamnit!' he cussed when he spotted a group of townspeople who looked as though

23

they were some kind of delegation. Miss Agatha Webb was with them and she was pointing in his direction. The group was led by a man in a black suit sporting a stiff white collar, Pastor Webb no doubt. The delegation started towards him.

'You've got a welcoming committee, Mr Noah,' Polly drawled.

He did not reply. He studied the group of boys lounging at the far end of the platform who were laughing raucously as they passed a jug around the group. They had also spotted him, he saw. Some were laughing whilst others made crude gestures and a few were even shaking their fists.

'Seems like trouble is headed your way, Mr Noah,' Miz Polly drawled.

'You ain't the only one feeling like a fish out of water, Miz Polly,' he rejoined.

'These folk seem to be expecting you, Mr Noah,' she observed.

'They're expecting the new schoolteacher, a young gent called Mr Noah. He passed away in Flannigan's bar. Maybe you noticed him.'

'He bought my ticket west, Mr Noah.'

'You went through a dead man's pockets?'

'So did you Mr Noah. So did you. You took his ticket.' She paused. 'Maybe you had best keep your lips buttoned, Mr Noah. Besides which no one will believe you ain't the schoolteacher. They will just assume you aim to save your hide.'

'What do you mean, Miz Poll?'

'Hell, Mr Noah, one of those young varmints is carrying a bullwhip. I guess you are their target. It'll be interesting to see if any of those good folk have the stomach to stand up to those young varmints! Not that you'll need them. You're a mean-hearted varmint, Mr Noah! Pure poison, I've heard it said!'

'I could say the same about you, Miz Polly.'

'Welcome, Mr Noah,' the pastor called. 'Welcome to our town.'

This foolishness had gone on long enough. He was damned if he wanted to be Mr Noah, respectable schoolteacher. He was Noah Swan, bartender! He needed to get back to where he belonged. He needed to find a saloon, preferably one that wasn't fool enough to employ Miz Polly. That woman was poison and dangerous.

The words stuck in his craw. The welcoming delegation stood as if rooted. They were all staring at the approaching group of boys. He could almost smell their fear. And he knew damn well that if there was going to be trouble not one of these gents would step forward to save the town's new 'schoolteacher'.

The large boy leading the band uttered a bloodcurdling whoop. He was the boy holding the bullwhip. Realization dawned. The no-good young varmint did indeed plan to use the whip on his new schoolteacher. Noah knew that the young man who had died in Flannigan's Bar would have stood no chance at all, he would not have been able to prevent himself being cut to ribbons.

From the corner of his eye he saw Pastor Webb take his startled sister by the arm. There was no need for that, Noah decided. Miss Agatha would not be rushing to his rescue. She'd covered her eyes with her hands, which just confirmed what he had known all along. She was not his kind of woman!

'Looks like you're going to get your just deserts, Mr Noah!' Miz Polly folded her arms over her ample bosom. 'Do you need help? I can throw an accurate blade!'

'So can I, Miz Polly. So can I. You keep out of this. I've a hunch that if you stick that young galoot between the eyes you'll fetch the whole damn town down on us. I know what you are capable of, Miz Polly. But the folk here don't. Better for you it stays that way.'

'Damn schoolteacher! You ain't wanted in

this town,' Freddy Black bellowed. He had been looking forward to this moment with great anticipation. His pa, Theodore Black, was busy hanging a man and the lard barrel of a lawman was snoozing in his office. He knew no one would interrupt his fun.

He was surprised to see that the schoolteacher did not look scared. Nor did he look very much like a schoolteacher. There was a hard-eyed look about this man that caused Freddy a moment of unease. But he couldn't back down now. He'd told the other boys what he was going to do. If he turned tail and fled they would brand him a yellow quitter!

'I don't give a damn,' Noah drawled.

'Get on with it, Freddy! Whip him good!' The boys stamped their feet. They shouted and whooped. And no one made a move to drive the young varmints from the station platform.

Noah's eyes narrowed. He kept his eyes fixed on the arm that would wield the lethal bullwhip.

For a moment the boy called Freddy hesitated. And then, with a blood-curdling whoop, he threw back his arm before bringing the bullwhip down hard against the wooden slats of the platform.

Freddy had seen his pa reduce a man to red

meat with this very bullwhip. He couldn't understand why the new schoolteacher didn't stumble backwards in terror. The man just stood there, his face remained expressionless.

Noah knew the young idiot was not within striking distance. He'd seen bullwhips in action and even knew how to use one himself. He intended to use this very same whip to drive these boys from the platform. None, he saw, was carrying a shooter. Which meant he wouldn't need to kill any of them! He'd do it. If his own life were in danger! It didn't occur to him for a second that he wouldn't be able to handle the likes of Freddy.

Freddy Black stepped forward. He had been practising using the whip when his pa was not around. He tried to judge the distance. He took another step forward, and then, bringing his arm back he sent the whip snaking forward. His target was the schoolteacher's face.

Instinctively Noah threw up an arm to shield his face. He felt the bite of the whip through his coat and knew his blood would ooze through the coat. He waited.

Freddy was surprised; the schoolteacher had not made a sound nor crumbled. With a grin he sent the whip snaking forward again.

Noah lunged and managed to catch hold of the whip. Bracing his feet he jerked viciously, hauling the whip and the young varmint who still clung hold of it in his direction. The boy was getting off lightly. Noah could think of any number of galoots who would have blasted the young idiot without a second thought.

Without a word he head-butted young Freddy with all the force he could muster. Freddy fell to the ground, unconscious and no longer any kind of threat. Noah had the bullwhip now and intended making good use of it. He advanced on the young no-goods, sending the whip snaking forward. They were running now, screaming when the whip cracked against flesh, fleeing from the station as though the devil himself were on their heels. He didn't pursue them. He was content to watch as they made their escape. As far as he was concerned they had learned a valuable lesson today. Maybe next time they'd stop and think before going after someone who had done them no harm.

He turned towards the welcoming delegation. They all wore stunned expressions. Pastor Webb's face wore an expression of horror and so did that of his sister. It occurred to Noah that no one would come forward to congratulate him on a job well done, which said something about this town. Noah could almost smell the fear.

'You have knocked Theodore Black's son out cold,' a man said almost accusingly as he knelt beside the insensible boy.

Noah shrugged. 'So!' he essayed.

'This is Theodore Black's town.' A citizen seemed eager to supply this information. 'He is the biggest rancher in these parts. No one crosses Theodore Black!'

'Too bad,' Noah drawled. 'It does us all good to be crossed from time to time!' He paused, 'I take it none of you good folk will be welcoming me to Hawk's Head. No matter! I was not anticipating a welcome.' Nor had he been expecting trouble.

A middle-aged woman bustled forward. 'Come with me, Mr Noah, I'll show you the schoolhouse. There is a freshly baked pie waiting for you. You will have to forgive us but you have taken us all by surprise. I'm Dora Wallace. My late husband ran the town's paper and now I'm doing my best to follow in his footsteps.'

He could always set them straight about his true identity another day. Hell, he just could not be bothered trying to deny he was the schoolteacher.

'Mr Black will not be pleased with you,' she warned. 'There may be trouble!'

He knew damn well there would be further trouble. 'We'll stop by the general store on the way to the schoolhouse. If you don't object,' he replied, not giving a damn whether she objected or not. He realized that it was imperative to get hold of a shotgun. If Theodore Black came calling he would be prepared.

'This way.' Mrs Dora Wallace steered him down Main Street. The saloon was easy to spot. And so was its garish sign. Black's Saloon, it read.

'Tell me about this town, ma'am. I am curious.'

'Well, it was founded by Theodore Black's grandfather,' she replied. 'So naturally Mr Black is an important man. His ranch is the largest in the territory and he also owns the saloon.' She paused. 'So teaching is your vocation, Mr Noah?' she essayed curiously.

A commotion on Main Street caused him to turn around and look back towards Black's Saloon. He had forgotten about Miz Polly. It seemed she was not faring well.

'Get out of here, you no-account long-in-the-tooth old...' a smartly suited overweight *hombre* sporting a handlebar moustache

31

yelled. With a shove he sent Polly flying through the batwings. She sprawled on Main Street. She had landed, Noah saw, upon horse droppings.

He did not laugh. Nor did he go to help her. She would not have appreciated him seeing her humiliation. To his surprise a Chinese woman came running out from the laundry. She helped Polly to her feet and guided her quickly inside. The town, it seemed, had one Good Samaritan.

'Who is that galoot?' Noah indicated the saloon boss who now lounged against the wall of the saloon, a lighted cigar clamped between his lips.

'His name is Edgar Smith. He manages the saloon for Theodore Black.'

Noah nodded. Edgar Smith had made a mistake, and in due time he'd find out. But it wasn't his concern. Working in Black's Saloon was out of the question, so he would not be obliged to save the man's life. Polly was as dangerous as any man. She'd be out for revenge. She'd wait for an opportunity. Edgar Smith was a dead man.

'So what happened to the last teacher?' he asked.

'Why, I believe he found a better-paid position,' Mrs Wallace answered quickly.

'Is that so?' He wasn't fooled.

'That is what Theodore Black says happened,' she answered. 'And that is what my paper printed. This is Mr Noah, our new schoolteacher.' She introduced him as they stepped into the general store.

'What can I get you, Mr Noah?' the storekeeper asked. 'You'll need a cane, I expect.'

'Nope.' Noah shook his head. 'What I need is a good shotgun.'

'You ain't going to use a shotgun on your pupils, are you, Mr Noah?' the storekeeper joshed uneasily.

'I'm a peaceful man,' Noah replied. 'And no I won't be blasting my pupils. The shotgun is reserved for real hardcases, not young ones pretending to be hardcases.'

'Seems like you and real hardcases ain't strangers, Mr Noah,' the storekeeper essayed as he placed a shotgun on the counter.

'I'm a peaceful man,' Noah replied. 'I try to avoid trouble.'

'Unfortunately young Freddy Black threatened Mr Noah with violence,' Mrs Wallace explained. 'Mr Noah was entirely blameless, but of course Theodore Black may not see things that way. He dotes on his boy!'

There was sudden commotion out on Main Street. Noah heard the words, 'lynching' and the name of someone called Dobbs.

A farmer burst into the store. 'Theodore Black has lynched Dobbs! Caught him red-handed with the beef.'

'Sounds like Mr Black is a law unto himself. In this town, then, a man can hang another with impunity!'

'Hell, no. But Dobbs was fool enough to be caught stealing beef.'

'How many?'

'Just the one.'

'I understand.' And so he did. This truly was Theodore Black's town.

Theodore Black looked at Freddy. He studied the bruise spreading over his son's forehead. He knew his son had only himself to blame.

Theodore himself, if threatened with a bullwhipping, would have blasted whoever wielded the whip. The schoolteacher was blameless.

'Are you going to blast him, Pa?' Freddy croaked.

'What I'm going to do is have words with this Mr Noah. You count yourself lucky to be still breathing, you and your fool no-account so-called friends who ran for their lives at the crack of a whip.' He paused before continuing angrily. 'You had no business going after the new schoolteacher. One of these days you're gonna go a step too far and I won't be around to help you. What a damn position you have put me in. For once in my life I just ain't sure what I am going to do. This town needs a schoolteacher. If I run him out I'll have a hell of a lot of folks bad-mouthing me.' He rubbed his chin. The town could always get another schoolteacher. He guessed Mr Noah would have to go, because if he didn't folk would always remember how the schoolteacher had knocked Theodore Black's boy out cold and got away with it.

'Thank you kindly, ma'am.' They had arrived at the schoolhouse.

'You are welcome, Mr Noah.' She hesitated. 'I'll bring you round one of my homemade pies, a welcome to Hawk's Head if you like.'

'Thank you, ma'am.'

'Being a widow is a lonely state of affairs, Mr Noah.' When he did not reply she continued hurriedly, 'I don't blame you for doing what you did. Young Freddy Black is a disgrace. And so is that creature we saw on Main Street. Why, I have a good mind to ask the sheriff to run her out of town.'

'No, ma'am, that wouldn't be a good idea. Folk that stick their noses into matters not their concern are liable to get them cut off.' Hell, Polly would be capable of that kind of deed. 'Now you get along home.' He paused. 'I'll look forward to that pie.'

'Of course, Mr Noah.' Blushing, she hurried away. He hoped for her sake she'd forgotten about getting Polly run out of town.

As Theodore Black walked towards the schoolhouse he was aware that most of the town was following him. He walked slowly with measured steps. A handful of his men walked with him. He was still angry with Freddy, not so much angry that Freddy had gone after the schoolteacher but angry that Freddy had so misjudged the kind of man the schoolteacher had turned out to be. Freddy had shown flawed judgement and out here this was particularly dangerous. He stopped outside the schoolhouse and raised his voice.

'Come on out, teacher! I want a word with you.' He was curious to see how the man Mr Noah reacted to the challenge. Men who knew what he was capable of would be shaking in their boots. The new man in town didn't sound the kind to shake in his boots. Inexplicably it occurred to Theodore that this man might be his equal.

Noah picked up the shotgun. He was back in familiar territory, obliged to confront a troublemaker, to avert trouble if he could but if not to see it through to the end. Whatever the end might be!

Hell, he ought to have seen the trouble with Elmore Standish through to the end. What the hell had he been thinking about, boarding a train headed for the frontier! He took a deep breath and then opened the schoolhouse door. Noah himself was a loner and so he found it hard to understand why Black had felt the need to bring most of the town along with him and men who were obviously part of his hard-bitten crew.

'It looks like you are no stranger to that shotgun, Mr Noah,' Black essayed. 'I never reckoned teaching school to be a man's job! I'm here to run you out of town, Mr Noah.'

'I figured that might be the case. It's been a long day for both of us, Mr Black. You've been busy hanging a man who stole your beef and I've been stuck on a train unable to stretch my legs. Why don't we take the easy way out? Toss a coin. And let's be done with it. We're both reasonable men!'

'Why the hell should we toss a coin?'

'I've no wish to kill folk in this town, Mr

Black. If you wanted a shootout you should have come solo. There are women and young ones in the crowd that has followed along behind you, hoping for free entertainment. Naturally you would be my target but...' Noah shrugged.

'You're threatening my people!'

'Staying alive is what I do best,' Noah rejoined. 'Folk will soon forget about the day Mr Noah was blasted but they won't forget if he took young ones and womenfolk with him. Your name will remain tarnished for a mighty long time. They'll blame you and young Freddy!'

'Your letter applying for the job stated you abhor violence.'

'Well, so I do. That's why I think you ought to toss a coin.'

'For a man who abhors violence you seem mighty good at dishing it out!'

'I've been around, Mr Black. I do what it takes to stay alive!' He would have said more but at that moment a slug embedded itself in the schoolhouse wall.

'Goddamn you! Goddamn you,' the boy yelled. But before he could shoot again townsmen fell on him, wrestling him to the ground.

'What the hell!' Noah exclaimed, part of his

mind thinking that none of these townsfolk had been eager to fall upon a whip-wielding Freddy Black. Then they had just stood and stared as though transformed to stone.

'Goddamn scum!' Black exclaimed. 'I ought to have hung him along with his pa.'

Realization dawned. This boy was kin to the hanged man, the luckless Dobbs.

'We'll do it now. No one takes a shot at Theodore Black and gets away with it!'

The boy had been hauled to his feet. He was smaller and scrawnier than Freddy Black. He was a damn bad shot as well, Noah reflected grimly. Clearly no one in this town was going to speak up and tell Black that it was not right to hang this boy. Which meant he would have to do it, Noah realized. He found himself hoping the boy was not as dim-witted as he looked nor as dim-witted as he'd behaved in attempting murder in full view of a good many citizens.

'Now hold your horses,' Noah yelled. 'I reckon I have a say in this matter.'

'You! What the hell are you talking about? This matter has nothing to do with you, schoolteacher.' The contemptuous way Black spat out the word schoolteacher told Noah plenty.

'It's got plenty to do with me,' Noah stood

39

his ground. 'If I can overlook a boy who damn near tried to whip me to death I can sure overlook a boy who's taken a bad shot at me.'

'Why the hell would anyone want to shoot at you,' someone yelled.

'Why the hell would a young galoot come at me with a bullwhip,' Noah rejoined. 'I'm damned if I know. But I've let one young varmint get away with it and I am inclined to extend my generosity to this one also. Let him go, I say. Let him run home to his ma and that will be an end to the matter.' The boy, much to his relief, kept his mouth shut.

'What if I say different,' Theodore Black challenged.

'Do you say different, Mr Black?' Noah asked. 'Because if you do we have one hell of a problem to resolve. It's up to you. I'm ready to meet my maker, ready to spit in his eye for dealing out dud cards. Can you say the same?'

CHAPTER 3

Theodore Black stared at the schoolteacher. The man wasn't a stranger to trouble, that was for sure. When facing death it was natural to call for help. Lord help me, men said. What this man had said had shaken Theodore.

'Howdy there, ladies. Surely you can persuade Mr Black to show mercy!'

The ladies didn't respond directly but Theodore could hear them whispering to one another. They were respectable women-folk. If any of them were shot down today the blame would be laid at his door. He sensed the man wasn't bluffing. Theodore could not afford to have his name tarnished in this way.

Noah wondered whether the rancher would call his bluff. Well, he would soon find out.

Theodore acknowledged to himself that this crazy varmint had nothing to lose and was more than capable of blasting women-folk. Out here on the frontier that was the most heinous of crimes. The schoolteacher was a no-account bum, whereas he himself was a successful rancher in the process of building up a cattle empire. He had a son to think about. If he were to die today it would all have been for nothing. Freddy was still a kid. He wouldn't be able to keep the ranch afloat. Things would start turning bad and Lord knew what would become of Freddy.

He smiled but the smile did not reach his eyes. 'It looks like this is your lucky day.' He addressed the Dobbs boy. 'Now you run along home to your ma!' He paused. 'But I give you fair warning, if you try anything like this again you will hang. Now get out of my sight!'

Noah wasn't fooled. He stared at that fixed smile, aware that inwardly the man was seething with rage. A big-shot rancher such as this man would be unaccustomed to being challenged.

'Thank you, Mr Noah,' the terrified boy croaked, before bolting.

Noah acknowledged the thanks with a brief nod. He continued to regard Theodore Black. He knew enough about folk to know that he'd made an enemy. Thanks to young Freddy the two of them had got off on the wrong foot. Matters could not be set right.

This man was not worried about meddling

in matters that were not his concern, Theodore Black thought savagely. This wasn't over between them. He knew it and he guessed the schoolteacher did likewise. The rancher kept his smile fixed in place. 'Well, I will bid you good day then, Mr Noah.' He paused. 'The town expects results. Don't let us down!'

Mrs Dora Wallace, who had been on the perimeter of the crowd realized that Mr Noah was a dangerous man. She found him attractive.

Miss Agatha Webb, who had also been on the perimeter of the crowd with her brother, realized Mr Noah was not the man she had thought him to be.

Next morning Mrs Wallace left home at a very early hour. As a respectable woman she couldn't risk being seen on the sidewalks once darkness had fallen. Her rendezvous with Mr Noah would therefore take place before the majority of folk were up and about. A bright red-and-white squared cloth covered the pie she had baked especially for him. And it was a sound reason for dropping by!

Noah woke early. He sat in the kitchen with a jug of freshly brewed coffee. This two-bit town had but the one saloon and that was owned by Theodore Black. Hell, he could not work for Black. He either had to take the schoolteaching job or head out. Undecided he tossed a coin and the fall of the coin told him to stay awhile. He found himself hoping that none of the little varmints would turn up for school today. He would prefer it that way. He didn't object to being paid for doing nothing. He had a bad feeling about this town. He belonged in a city. So what the hell was he doing here! A loud persistent knocking at the door interrupted his reflections. He wondered who it was.

'Here's your pie, Mr Noah. As promised,' Mrs Dora Wallace trilled brightly. He stared at the pie. The truth was he had forgotten about the woman and her pie! The only woman he was likely to remember was Miz Polly and that was because she was a viper that could strike at any time. Like himself she was a survivor. Hell, he wondered how she liked life at the laundry. There would be no saloon work for her here. He guessed the laundry was preferable to being in the gutter.

'Let me cut you a piece.' Mrs Wallace saw that his mind was elsewhere. 'Now, Mr Noah, if you are thinking of running me out of this schoolhouse you must think again. I am here to welcome you to Hawk's Head!' She paused. 'In a way you won't forget.'

Mrs Wallace wasn't a young woman, so perhaps she knew what she was doing.

'I ain't the marrying kind, Mrs Wallace.'

'Good Lord. I am not proposing, Mr Noah!'

He smiled. 'I know better than to argue with a determined woman.'

At the laundry Polly stifled a curse. Her rescuer had brought her a mug of coffee and a bowl of porridge. Polly glared at the unappealing stuff before managing to summon a smile. She couldn't even begin to pronounce the woman's name but it sounded similar to Anna so Anna she was going to be. She chewed the porridge, forcing it down. 'I'm no scrounger! I reckon I'll be helping out in the laundry until I am ready to move on.'

Edgar Smith was going to get what was coming! She would bide her time until the moment was right. So for now she was reduced to washing stinking dudes belonging to worthless no-account varmints. Hell, who would have thought it!

'I shall bake you another pie. I'll bring it

over tomorrow.'

Noah nodded. 'I look forward to your visit, ma'am.' He watched as she hurried down Main Street and then decided to take a stroll around town himself. He sure as hell didn't feel obliged to turn up at school prompt on time. Nor did he give a damn whether his pupils turned up on time, or not at all.

McGraph came out of the saloon feeling as though someone was hammering inside his head. He blinked. His throat was parched. Yesterday he had passed out inside Black's Saloon. Edgar Smith had left him be, for he was a good customer. The Irishman stuck his head into the horse trough. That helped. Yesterday he remembered how Edgar had thrown an old floozie out of the saloon. He remembered seeing her being helped into the laundry. He couldn't have explained why he did it but he found himself lurching towards the laundry.

There wasn't any sign of the woman. Tubs of hot water had been readied and piles of stinking dudes lay around waiting to be washed. Occasionally the *hombres* in this town tried to put a scare into the tiny woman who ran the laundry. With a whoop McGraph sent a tub of hot water spilling over the floor as he let rip with a string of profanities.

Polly, coming into the laundry room with a cigar clamped firmly between her lips, arrived just in time to see the large black-haired man send the tub flying. She didn't even stop to think, she reacted instinctively.

McGraph caught the whiff of a strong cigar. He turned and saw the large red-headed woman, face contorted with rage, but even so he didn't realize her intention. With considerable force Polly struck the still befuddled varmint across the side of the head with a scrubbing board. The scrubbing board continued to fall, striking him across the shoulders with force. Profaning, McGraph on his hands and knees crawled from the laundry.

'You polecat,' she yelled, planting a kick on his rear end.

McGraph lurched to his feet still profaning. He reached for his pistol hardly aware of what he was doing. A howl of pain left his lips as something hard struck his wrist. The weapon fell from his nerveless fingers.

'Don't do anything foolish,' a voice drawled.

Holding his broken wrist McGraph saw the town's new schoolteacher, that interfering varmint Mr Noah!

Noah returned the fool's stare. Hell, he might have saved the man's life. He knew darn well Miz Polly always carried a blade.

He raised his voice. 'Don't let me catch any more of you varmints messing with this laundry. Leave this laundry be! Next time I catch any troublemakers disturbing my morning stroll I aim to shoot first and talk later.' He paused. 'Understood?'

'Hell, this is nothing to do with you, Mr Noah!' the man snarled.

'Get out of my sight, you varmint. I'm a peaceful schoolteacher and you've forced me to resort to violence. Get out of my sight before I finish you off for good.'

As the man stumbled away, Miz Polly sauntered towards Noah. 'You're a damn liar, Mr Noah,' she hissed. 'Peaceful school-teacher indeed!'

'Well, I don't expect any thanks for saving your neck, Miz Polly,' he rejoined mildly.

'Saving my neck? What the hell are you talking about?'

'Hell, Miz Polly, you can't put a knife through a man's heart before the eyes of the town. Why, I reckon Hawk's Head would want to hang you from the nearest tree. Yep, I've saved your necky, Miz Polly. I guess it would be too much to expect free laundry.'

'It would and don't expect me to save your hide, Mr Noah, when trouble comes calling. You've made enemies, Mr Noah.' She paused. 'But I'll bear in mind what you say.'

'About what?'

'Why, about knifing any no-account bums before the eyes of this two-bit town.'

'Amen to that, Miz Polly. If you restrain yourself it will save me one hell of a lot of trouble. I ain't got a mind to come to your rescue every time you forget that your neck will snap the same as any other neck once the noose goes over your head.'

'Why the hell would you want to come to my rescue, Mr Noah?' she demanded. 'We ain't never...'

'Well, you and me, Miz Polly. We go back a long time. We've both passed too many years at Flannigan's Bar. We ain't the adventurous sort, Miz Polly. We've stayed stuck in a rut for far too long. And now we've both ended up in this no-account town!'

'You don't fool me, Mr Noah. You're wishing yourself back at Flannigan's. Ain't that a fact?'

'And you're wishing yourself some place else, anywhere but the laundry.' He paused. 'I'll be dropping by with my laundry if that's all right with you.'

'Well, I ain't one to turn custom away. Say, Mr Noah, why the hell is that woman glaring our way. If looks could kill I'd be done for.'

He turned his head. Mrs Dora Wallace was indeed glaring their way.

'What's going on between you two?' Polly essayed. 'Your ears have turned red!'

'Nothing, Miz Polly, nothing at all.' He hurried away.

Mrs Dora Wallace couldn't control herself. She rushed across Main Street.

'I know the sheriff. You're an undesirable. I'll see to it you're run out of this town. We don't want your kind in Hawk's Head!'

'Hell, you've been up to hanky-panky with Mr Noah.' Polly planted her hands on her hips. 'You back off or I'm going to start yelling out what you've been doing with the town's new schoolteacher.' She paused. 'And don't think you're going to get him to the altar. He ain't that much of a fool. Now get. Before I let the whole town know what you two have gotten up to.' She winked. 'Him and me have just come to an understanding!' And so they had. He'd be bringing his laundry.

Face crimson, shaking with fury, Dora Wallace spun on her heels.

Noah entered the classroom. He sat down at his desk. He gazed at the row of empty desks confronting him. Soon the little varmints would be arriving, expecting to be taught their letters. He began to alter the set-up of the tables. He set them out as he would have expected them to be set out in a saloon.

'Like you said, Mr Noah, we go back along way!' a voice exclaimed.

'Hell, Miz Polly, are you signing up for lessons?'

'I'm just here to tell you your predecessor, Edward White, well, he just disappeared one day. Word was he had upped and left but no one saw him leave.' She winked. 'Anna keeps her ears open.'

'Anna?'

'The only one to give me a helping hand, Mr Noah, when Edgar Smith made the biggest damn mistake of his miserable life.' She paused, 'Anna reckons Clem Sawyer, our no-account lawman, knows a lot more than has been said about Edward White. It was common knowledge in town that the youngsters were making his life hell; in particular young Freddy Black took great pleasure in baiting the young Easterner. And that, Mr Noah, is all I can tell you. I wish you good day.' With that she was gone.

Clem Sawyer the lawman made no attempt to prevaricate. He continued to lounge on his chair, booted feet resting against the cigar-burnt desk. 'So you've got wind of what happened to that damn fool White,' he replied. 'He ought to have known he was not suited to life in a frontier town. Why, some of those varmints attending school are almost grown men. They gave him hell, Mr Noah, and the worst of them was Freddy Black. But you know that.'

'I reckon.' Uninvited, Noah sat down. 'Are you going to tell me what really happened to White?'

'Sure I can tell you what I know, but from what I've heard you ain't likely to suffer a similar fate!'

'And what fate might that be?'

'Well there ain't much to tell. When he disappeared I rode out searching for the varmint just in case he'd lost himself. I had to do it. Mrs Brannigan, one of the parents, was giving me hell so to shut her up I rode out.' The lawman paused before continuing, 'I found him but I was too late. He'd been tarred and feathered and left to die out there in the sun. He wasn't capable of making it back to town on foot.'

'And you did nothing?'

'I covered him up, got him into the buggy and got him back to town. I got him over to the undertaker. We buried him discreetly. I got Pastor Webb to read a few words as we planted the luckless fool. And that was that. Theodore Black is a big wheel around town. There was no proof linking Freddy to the deed. And young Freddy has kept his trap shut; certainly he ain't been boasting about doing for the schoolteacher.'

'So you didn't want to cross Theodore Black.'

'Nope. Not without proof.' He shrugged. 'So far as I know he ain't hung an innocent man. He'd argue he's been saving the town the trouble of a trial.' The lawman paused, 'I'm getting on, Mr Noah, and yes, I am reluctant to tangle with Black and his hard-bitten crew. Next year I aim to take my pension and retire. Now if you've got anything further to say spit it out and then let me be.'

Noah shook his head. 'Nope, my business here is concluded. I guess I'll head back to school. Those little varmints will be kicking their heels!'

The lawman nodded. 'I ain't a fool, Mr Noah. Whatever you are you ain't no school-

teacher. A schoolteacher knows his place.
You've been tangling with folk in this town,
Mr Noah. You've made enemies. Theodore
Black is a man to carry a grudge, for as long
as it takes.'

'He ain't the only one.' Noah didn't elab-
orate. 'I ain't out to avenge Edward White. I
didn't even know the man. I aim to stay alive
any way I can. My only hope is that certain
folk in Hawk's Head will leave me in peace.
Now that ain't too much to ask?'

'Don't count on it, Mr Noah,' the lawman
advised.

Noah left the law office. Sure as hell he
could not count on the lawman. The man
was a disgrace. But then so were most folk.
From behind the bar Noah had seen all
kinds. And he had dealt with the likes of
Theodore Black many times over!

Slowly he made his way back to the schoolhouse. There were not that many pupils, to
be sure, but some had turned up. And so had
Pastor Webb and his sister Agatha.

'You're late!' the pastor accused, pulling
out his pocket watch. 'And the desks, you've
moved the desks!'

'Good morning, Miss Agatha.'

Miss Agatha clung to her brother's arm.
She did not return his greeting.

'Have you got anything else to tell me, Pastor?'

'No. What do you mean?'

'I mean, is there anything else I ought to know?' From the corner of his eye he saw Freddy Black dismount, secure his horse and then swagger into the schoolhouse. Yep, he reflected, Freddy was an unpleasant rotten little varmint who was relying on his pa to keep him safe. The fool had yet to realize that Theodore wasn't always going to be around. At Freddy's age Noah himself had been more than able to keep himself alive. He'd been living on the streets along with other feral youngsters. Hell, these young galoots in Hawk's Head might think they were trouble but they didn't know what trouble was.

'I would advise you to put the desks back as you found them. You will need to keep order if the children are to learn.'

'Don't worry, Pastor Webb. Keeping order is what I do. And as for the desks they are staying as I have put them. I'll wish you good day.'

'I'll see you on Sunday!'

'Wild horses wouldn't get me through the door of your church, Pastor Webb. You're not man enough to tell me what befell teacher White. You've kept the secret, you and a few more in this town.' He paused. 'I ain't making it my concern. Although I reckon the truth will come out eventually.'

CHAPTER 4

Young Freddy Black slouched into the classroom. His pa was still making him attend school, saying that no way did he want this town thinking his boy was afraid of the new schoolteacher. Eyeing Mr Noah hatefully he went to his place without speaking.

'How's your head, Freddy?' one of the older girls piped up.

'Shut your mouth.' Freddy rejoined.

Noah glared at them both and they looked away.

'Ain't we going to say prayers?' a boy asked. The same boy had been asking the same question for the last couple of weeks.

'Nope,' Noah rejoined. 'Get out your books.' He guessed the late Edward White had prayed in vain for rescue.

A boy slunk into the classroom, mumbling an apology for lateness.

'Take a seat.' Noah was never going to

whack anyone for being late. As he spoke he kept an eye on Freddy Black. Freddy smirked. A couple of Freddy's cronies likewise smirked, causing Noah to form the opinion that the young varmints knew something he darn well didn't. From experience in tending bar he had a hunch that trouble was heading his way. He had a nose for trouble and he could smell it now. Trouble was coming to his schoolroom and Freddy Black had something to do with it. What had that young polecat gone and done now? One day that fool boy was going to get himself blasted.

Polly had a nose for trouble. It had kept her alive. Leaning against the laundry, taking a chance to escape from the steam inside, she saw the three men emerge from Black's Saloon. She could see what they were, exhibitionists each and every one of them. They wanted to be noticed. They made sure they were, spreading out, putting distance between them as they strutted down Main Street, hands hovering close to the butts of their Colt .45s. They were killers, hired guns heading for a killing. It occurred to her that they might be headed for the school and Mr Noah.

Some of the girls were emerging from the saloon, rubbing their eyes as they gawked after the hired killers. Their nervous giggles irked her. So did the way that a few of them, hugging flimsy drapes over their shoulders, set out after the gunmen. She wanted to yell out that smart women kept away from a place where bullets would soon be flying, but she knew her warning would fall on deaf ears for these girls were young and foolish.

'You there!' she sprang forward gripping a girl fiercely about the arm, 'Who are they going after? Tell me!'

The girl tried to jerk free but failed, 'Why, I believe it is the schoolteacher, Mr Noah,' she eventually divulged.

'Damn fools!' Polly shook her head. 'Damn fools! Who paid them?' She tightened her grip. 'Tell me now before I shake it out of you.'

'Well, I am sure I cannot say. But his pa is a big man in these parts.'

Polly released the girl, who staggered after the others. Polly didn't even think to tag along to see the show although by now a good many other folk were doing just that. There wouldn't be much of a show. When Noah Swan was involved things were over and done with pretty damn quick. She wondered if Freddy's pa knew what the little skunk had done; probably not, but old man Black would find out soon enough.

Freddy Black had thought it a mighty fine idea. But now he was not so sure. He was feeling queasy, thinking that maybe he ought not to have done it. Either way his pa was bound to give him hell. He shifted uneasily on his chair. Mr Noah was staring at him.

'Got something to tell me, Freddy?' Noah essayed.

'I ain't done nothing,' Freddy croaked, as his ears turned bright red.

'Just as well, for I have a very long memory. But if you were to have done something and if you were to tell me now I could overlook the misdeed.' Noah waited. 'This one time.'

'I ain't done nothing.' Freddy scrambled to his feet and bolted for the door 'You go to hell, Mr Noah. You go to hell!' he yelled defiantly.

Freddy didn't go far. He dived into a nearby alleyway. He half-expected Mr Noah to give chase but that didn't happen. His courage, which had faltered in the schoolroom, began to return.

Noah guessed this was answer enough. He grabbed hold of one of Freddy's friends.

'Talk!' he yelled. 'Before I do you real harm.' The implied threat was enough to make the cowardly little skunk talk. 'Get the hell out of my sight.' A booted foot helped the young varmint on his way. 'The rest of you line up nice and orderly. Leave by the back door and make your way to the church. You stay there till your folk come to collect you.' He watched them go with relief, knowing that he had got them out just in time.

The three men swaggered to a halt in front of the school. For a while they amused themselves by yelling obscenities. They knew this town. They knew no one would challenge them, especially not Clem Sawyer, the town's useless lawman. They knew the schoolteacher had bested Freddy Black but he was nothing but a youngster hiding behind his pa's reputation.

They were damn fools. Dispassionately Noah observed their antics. That fool of a boy had hired drunken bums to come after him. Presumably there hadn't been any 'genuine' top guns in town, so Freddy had settled for these three. Too bad for them! They'd come here to the school to do him harm. He wasn't about to give them any second chance. His hands were steady as he lifted his shotgun. He didn't particularly feel much of anything as he walked to the door. He wasn't afraid, he wasn't vengeful; he was just doing what needed to be done. And he'd always been a damn fine shot. Back East he'd patronized a damn fine shooting club for gentlemen. He wasn't a gentleman but he'd had the money to get into the club.

He kicked the door open and stepped out, firing at his targets as he did so, knowing that their reactions would not be quick enough to save them.

One of them went down clutching his belly, blood trickling between his fingers. The other two, staggering back in clear astonishment, were beginning to reach. Automatically he aimed for a head and saw his target explode in a mess of blood and bone. The other one turned to run and Noah had no compunction about blasting him in the back. He went down, blood pooling beneath his body.

The smell of gun smoke and death hung in the air and people who had taken cover slowly emerged, expressions stunned.

Noah waited; sure as hell no one was coming forward to congratulate him on his escape from death. He heard a few mutters concerning the one who had been shot in the back. It was hard to credit but a few of the varmints were actually criticizing him for shooting the murderously inclined galoot in the back.

Freddy Black had emerged from an alleyway, an expression of disbelief and guilt written clearly on his face.

'What the hell is going on,' a voice bellowed. The sheriff shouldered his way through the crowd. As usual he had timed his arrival to coincide with the end of the 'excitement'.

Noah smiled grimly. Freddy had slipped back into the alleyway. Without bothering to answer the sheriff's damn fool question Noah headed for the alleyway. He'd thought of a way to teach that little varmint a very important lesson. Three men, if they could be called men, were dead on account of Freddy's foolishness. He knew Theodore was not behind this. The elder Black would have hired top guns, not these hopeless cases. Yep, young Freddy must have swiped his pa's money to pay for riffraff.

Clem Sawyer fell into step beside the schoolteacher. 'What do you aim to do?' he mumbled nervously.

Freddy Black crouched down behind a pile of rotting garbage. He never would have thought it would have turned out this way, with the schoolteacher blasting the men sent to kill him. Mr Noah was bound to work it out and now Freddy feared for his life. Mr Noah was crazy and wouldn't give a damn that Freddy's pa was a man to be feared. Freddy didn't even have a gun with him!

'Come on out, Freddy, before I come in shooting!' Noah yelled from the mouth of the alleyway.

'Hell! You can't kill Freddy Black!' Clem Sawyer was actually taking an interest. 'You ain't got no proof! You can't gun down an unarmed youngster.'

'The money those three will be carrying will be proof enough. Freddy Black won't get his just deserts today. He can cool his heels in your cell along with those three galoots he hired to kill me. He can stay put until his pa comes to town and collects him.'

'I can't lock him up.'

'I'm not giving you a choice. Just tell Black you were humouring a crazy man. I'm the one he'll come after, not you. Your hide will be safe.' Whistling softly Noah entered the alleyway. Freddy was shaking too much to put up any kind of fight so Noah hauled him out by the scruff of his neck.

'You and me are taking a walk to the jail,' he told the no-account youngster. He eyed the sheriff, 'Think you can manage to round up the other three?'

Clem Sawyer nodded reluctantly. The schoolteacher would not be able to humiliate big-shot rancher Black with impunity.

'I ain't done nothing,' Freddy lied.

'Freddy,' Noah sighed, 'your friend blabbed! You told more than one what you'd done. I know that. Pretty soon your pa will know the truth of the matter. Those fools are dead because of you! I think it only just you keep them company for a while. It will give you time to reflect upon what you did. You may walk out of that jail cell a wiser young man. For your sake I hope you do. You keep on this way and one day, well, you will find that that day is your last. Someone whom you have crossed will kill you. You can't hide behind your pa for ever.'

He propelled Freddy into the jail and shoved him into a cell. 'Stay put! You have company coming.'

Freddy backed into a corner as one by one the three dead men were dumped in the cell.

'He'll bawl him out but he won't give him a hiding,' the sheriff observed with a shake of his head as the connecting door between the cells and the office was closed. 'And he'll come after you for this, Mr Noah.

That's the way he thinks.'

'That boy's a troublemaker.'

'And you're used to troublemakers, aren't you, Mr Noah?' the sheriff suggested.

'I am,' Noah replied grimly. 'But I didn't come to this town looking for trouble. Fact is, I am here because I wanted to avoid trouble.' He shrugged. 'The next move is up to Theodore Black, and as for you, sheriff, some time soon I reckon you must come down from that fence you are sitting on. There's something rotten in this town. And I reckon the blame can be laid at your door. You've turned a blind eye and let Theodore Black go after wide-loopers dispensing his own kind of justice.'

'It seemed easier that way and most folk hereabout agree wideloopers should hang,' the sheriff replied. 'I don't reckon young Freddy had anything to do with what happened to the last schoolteacher. We both know Freddy ain't able to keep his lip buttoned. He ain't blabbed concerning Edward White.'

Noah shrugged. He didn't rate Clem Sawyer highly and he guessed the lawman knew it.

'Say, that new woman at the laundry sure has a temper. I like a woman with a temper!'

The lawman was eager to change the subject.

'Is that so!'

'Are you two acquainted?' the lawman enquired.

'Nope. We were travelling companions, that's all.'

'I may mosey over and make her acquaintance.' The sheriff frowned. 'After young Freddy has been taken home by his pa. Theodore will be here soon enough to get his son out of a stinking fly-infested cell.' He paused, 'Yep, that dead meat will be drawing them in like a magnet. Young Freddy will be having a hell of a time! But I reckon he deserves it. And maybe this time Theodore will rein him in and teach him to toe the line. But I wouldn't bet on either of them seeing sense. You'll need eyes in the back of your head, Mr Noah.'

'Well, I will bid you good day then.' Noah left the office. Folk were still standing around gawking at the jailhouse. Killing three men had caused a stir but Noah reckoned throwing Freddy in jail had caused a greater stir, which said a lot for this town.

Clem Sawyer lit a cigar. Clearly Mr Noah had killed before. Killing those three fools had not troubled the schoolteacher.

From the cell Freddy howled to be let out.

Sawyer ignored the ruckus. His thoughts turned to Miz Polly, a woman with a volatile temper, the only woman to interest him for a very long while.

Theodore Black returned to his ranch as dusk was falling, to be greeted by his ramrod. 'We've got trouble!' the man announced without preamble. 'It's young Freddy. Word is he paid three no-account bums to blast the schoolteacher.'

'What are you trying to tell me?' Theodore demanded. 'You're not trying to tell me Freddy has been hurt.'

'No. Nothing like that! But Mr Noah blasted the three no-account bums hired by Freddy.'

'Where's my son?'

'Locked up in a jail cell until you get around to collecting him. Mr Noah insisted upon it!'

Theodore swore long and loud. 'Saddle up. You and me, we're headed for town.'

'It's damn risky riding at night, boss,' Smithers, the ramrod, cautioned.

Theodore considered, for a moment. Reluctantly he nodded. 'We'll leave at first light.'

Once alone he opened his safe. There was a wad of bills missing. His son had thieved the money. The men he had hired hadn't been good enough to do the job. And Mr Noah was no schoolteacher, that was for sure.

'I've landed in hell,' Polly grumbled as Anna handed her a mug of tea. 'You ain't charging enough for the laundry.'

Anna nodded. 'They all give me bad time,' she replied.

'Well, things are different now I've landed here.' Polly gulped down the tea. 'Hell, I don't like it, but I aim to make the best of it. I'll see that they all pay the going rate. We ain't slaves and we ain't being treated like slaves!'

A pale-faced woman from Black's Saloon, toting an enormous bundle of washing, had just staggered into the laundry.

'Tell your boss,' Polly raised her voice, 'from now on we're charging by the size of the bundle.' There would be a ruckus but there wouldn't be anything she couldn't handle.

Theodore Black and his ramrod rode slowly into town. There were more folk than usual about at this early hour. Expectant faces turned in his direction. He guessed everyone knew his son had been thrown in to jail.

68

Hell! If Freddy had been determined upon this course of action why the hell couldn't he have found men able to do the job?

Edgar Smith appeared on the sidewalk, his face reddening with rage. Theodore employed the man because Edgar used his fists to keep the women and anyone else in line.

'Damn uppity women!' Edgar yelled as he caught sight of his boss. 'That old vixen at the laundry, well she's got ideas above her station. It seems she's running that goddamn laundry now! She's calling the shots!'

Theodore watched in some amazement as Edgar proceeded to smear dudes with horse-dung before stuffing them back into a sack. Then, smirking all over his face, he headed for the laundry.

Theodore frowned, then proceeded on his way to the jail.

'Here's another sack!' Edgar declared as he emptied the sticking dudes on the floor. 'Do you think you can manage, you no-account old whore?'

To his surprise she smiled. 'You are willing to pay the extra?'

Edgar nodded. 'I am, but I want to see you wash them. You. Not the other one.'

Polly picked up the clothes. 'No problem, sir,' she replied civilly.

'I'm gonna watch you wash those dudes!' he declared threateningly.

'Feel free.' She didn't seemed troubled by the stinking garments, which threw him somewhat as he'd expected an outburst from her. He guessed she knew when she had met her match.

Theodore knocked open the jailhouse door. Striding in he let rip with a string of profanities concerning Mr Noah and no-account lawmen.

Sawyer took the abuse without protest. It was what he had been expecting. He waited until Theodore ran out of steam before replying. 'I'm not tangling with Mr Noah because of Freddy. At heart that school-teacher is a killer. He has that look about him, that look I've seen before! Now get your boy and take him home. He's lucky to be alive. He is lucky Mr Noah did not turn on him. Why, Freddy is almost a grown man. I reckon it is time he begins to act like a man and that means not hiring guns who ain't up to the job. It means not bringing trouble into my town. It means thinking things through.'

'Quit yapping,' Theodore Black ordered curtly. 'I might have known you didn't have the guts to stand up to Mr Noah.' Still cussing he opened the door leading into the cellblock. The smell caused him to slap a bandanna over his mouth and nose. Black flies were already swarming over the three dead bodies placed in the cell alongside Freddy.

'Pa, what took you so long?' Freddy sobbed.

'What the hell do you mean by this, Sawyer?' Theodore rounded on the sheriff, who had followed in his wake.

'Like I said. I ain't crossing Noah. He's got that loco look in his eye all natural born killers possess.'

'Straighten your shoulders, son,' Theodore yelled. 'You are walking out of here with your head held high.' He ignored the craven lawman, having sense enough to know that turning on Sawyer would make matters a damn sight worse as Sawyer was the one wearing the badge.

'I don't think I can, Pa.' Freddy grizzled as his pa helped him into the office. 'My legs are gonna give way.'

'So help me, Freddy, if you don't stiffen your spine and hold your head high I'm mighty tempted to leave you here. You never listen! Goddamnit! I told you I would deal with Noah in my own good time. Now we're

71

walking out of here. You and me! And if you shame the name of Black I'll boot you all the way down Main Street myself.'

CHAPTER 5

Noah wasn't foolish enough to believe that there was not going to be further trouble. He would not have been surprised to see a raging Theodore Black on his doorstep demanding that he step out and haul iron.

This did not occur. Black took his son straight home. He did not return to town and a week or so later Freddy slunk back into school. Noah didn't comment. To any casual observer things were calm in Hawk's Head, but Noah had enough savvy to know that beneath this calm surface anger simmered.

He'd heard that that fool Edgar Smith was making a habit of baiting Miz Polly. Any day now, any day now he thought, she'd strike and Smith would find out what he was dealing with. Smith had taken to referring to her as old Polly. It would be interesting, Noah thought, to see just how that devious woman dealt with her tormentor. By now she'd have something in mind; that was for sure.

When Edgar Smith strolled into the laundry he interrupted the Chinese proprietor midway through screeching at Polly. Edgar heard enough to learn that Polly was making a habit of taking a bottle of rotgut into the alleyway and getting damn drunk every night. The woman fell silent when she saw Edgar, gave a respectful bow, and disappeared into the back of the laundry.

'Get scrubbing, Polly,' Edgar ordered with a smirk. Putting two and two together he was mighty glad to realize he was the cause of her drunkenness. He'd driven her to it. To his great delight she did as ordered with a cowed expression on her face. Despite the stench of the dudes he'd brought in he could smell the stink of whiskey that hung about her. Proof, not that it was needed, that she was hitting the bottle real bad. He began to think about the alleyway. Various ideas just popped into his head.

From the mean look in his little pig eyes she knew she had been right concerning his character and the kind of rotten varmint he was at heart. Edgar Smith would be checking out the alleyway tonight. His intention no doubt would be to give her a good kicking whilst she lay insensible. The product of a city filled with riffraff, Polly knew darn well what certain varmints were capable of. Indeed, she'd staggered the streets inebriated and she could see now that she'd been darn lucky. Since arriving in Hawk's Head she had not touched a drop of rotgut whiskey. Most of the time when she had not been scrubbing clothes she'd been thinking of Edgar Smith, the galoot who'd sent her sprawling in muck. And she'd also come to realize that she and Anna could make a profit from the laundry. Those varmints in this town might have given Anna a bad time but Miz Polly didn't give a damn about any of them. She'd dealt with worse galoots than the men of Hawk's Head! And tonight she aimed to deal with Smith. The damn fool had taken the bait.

Edgar Smith passed his evening filled with anticipation. It was hard to wait whilst the hours of evening passed. He damn well hoped she would stick to what had sounded like her usual routine. It was late when he left the saloon quietly, but the saloon was still busy. Men with money always wanted liquor and women, generally in that order. He slipped out of the side entrance. The sidewalk was dark and deserted. Filled with anticipation he headed for the nearest alleyway to the laundry.

'Dear Lord, let her be there,' he muttered in a parody of prayer. And his prayer was answered. In the fetid darkness he heard her murmuring incoherently to herself.

She heard him coming, cussing when he stepped on filth. Beneath her dark cloak she held the long, wickedly sharp blade she'd carried around with her for years, ever since she'd been obliged to make her way in a dangerous world. She was a big woman and strong and she'd been obliged previously to use her blade. She could move quickly when she had to. A dark shape emerged from the darkness.

Her voice was low, 'Evening, Edgar.' Before he could gather his wits she sprang forward.

When she left the alleyway, Main Street was still deserted. She slipped into the laundry. Two hot tubs stood ready. One for her! One for her clothes! She smiled. Edgar Smith would not be troubling her again. He had received his just deserts.

As daylight broke McGraph lurched out of the saloon, stumbled into an alleyway and heaved up the contents of his stomach. He was still vomiting when he spotted the fancy red boots sticking out from behind a pile of garbage. His befuddled mind did not at first associate the red boots with Edgar Smith. He lurched to investigate.

What he saw was something he would never forget. Smith's stomach had been slit wide open. The man's innards had tumbled out. And if that wasn't enough Smith's throat had been slit from ear to ear. Uttering a strangled yell McGraph drew his .45 and fired into the air. He stumbled out on to Main Street and discharged the weapon until the chamber was empty.

'What the hell?' Clem Sawyer appeared on Main Street. The lawman was dishevelled with his shirt unfastened and his feet minus their boots.

Polly heard the commotion outside. Inside the laundry it was work as usual. The tubs were steaming. She and Anna were just drinking their tea before they got scrubbing. Neither woman said a word concerning the commotion.

Noah came out on to Main Street when he heard the shouting and yelling and the sound of shooters being discharged. He pushed his way through the milling crowd and stared down at the luckless Edgar Smith. Around him folk were speculating about who had done for Smith. The names of enemies were bandied around, men who might have harboured a grudge.

Noah said nothing. Naturally enough no one mentioned Miz Polly. He didn't enlighten them. That damn fool Smith should have known better than to underestimate a woman like Miz Polly. If she'd been a man she would have made him haul iron but... Shaking his head Noah turned away.

Clem Sawyer, who was being pressed to do something, reluctantly announced that every building in town was to be searched in the hope of maybe rooting out bloodstained dudes. Men eager to go along with the idea started the search. Noah watched. No one thought to search the laundry. Noah knew they would not find any bloodstained dudes there in any event. Yep, they would have been washing late last night!

Idly he wondered how Miz Polly had got Edgar into that stinking alleyway. Presumably he walked willingly into the trap.

'What about the saloon women!' a waddy said. 'Ain't you going to question them?'

'You damn fool,' Sawyer rejoined. 'You show me a woman able to bring down a powerfully built *hombre* like Smith and I'll take my hat off to her. This is a man's work. Say Mr Noah, where were you last night?'

'Not at the saloon,' Noah replied curtly. 'I've no quarrel with Edgar Smith. Since arriving in Hawk's Head I have not set foot in Black's Saloon.'

Sawyer nodded. 'Even so I guess I must search the schoolhouse. No offence intended, but there cannot be an exception.'

'Go ahead.' Noah folded his arms. He lounged against a post. 'If you've no objection I will wait here. Let me know when you have finished.' He watched the fools hurrying around, watched whilst the remains of Smith were bundled into a blanket and carried to the undertaker's place.

Respectable womenfolk, whilst evidencing horror, seemed particularly interested in what was going on. The saloon girls, a gaggle of whom had appeared on the sidewalk, did not seem too put out at losing their boss.

'Mr Noah. Mr Noah.' The woman's voice was urgent. Turning his head Noah saw a careworn woman headed his way.

'Seems you are in demand!' Miz Polly sauntered out of the laundry. Her sleeves were tucked up to the elbows. He guessed she had already started work.

'I'm Mrs Brannigan.' The woman introduced herself. 'You teach my son.'

He nodded. 'Your boy is doing real well,

Mrs Brannigan. His reading and writing is progressing real well.'

'I'm not here to talk about Tom's reading and writing, Mr Noah,' she snapped. 'Although I am well pleased with your efforts.'

'So what's bothering you, ma'am?' he enquired.

'It's Tom. I've locked him in the cellar for his own good.'

'But what's that to do with me, ma'am?' Looking at the agitated woman he had a hunch he was about to be roped into something he wanted no part of.

'He was determined to ride out to the Glover place and look for young Dotty Glover. No one has seen her for some time. She ought to have been at school, Mr Noah!'

He shrugged. 'Since the fracas at the schoolhouse some folk might have deliberately kept pupils away.' He paused. 'I don't hunt them down, Mrs Brannigan, if they don't attend.'

She burst into tears.

'What the hell is going on?' Miz Polly exclaimed. 'Just what do you think will happen to your boy if he rides out to the Glover spread. Clearly you are afraid for his safety or you would not have come looking for Mr Noah!'

'If he goes anywhere near the Glover spread demanding to see Dotty I am afraid they are liable to give him a beating or maybe even shoot him.'

'*They,* Mrs Brannigan?' Noah queried.

'Seth Glover and his four sons.' Mrs Brannigan twisted her hands.

'Mr Noah will go,' Miz Polly volunteered. 'He's the schoolteacher after all. It's reasonable for him to enquire why a pupil has not been attending.'

'Now look here, Miz Polly!' he protested weakly.

'Do you want young Tom's death on your conscience, Mr Noah?' She winked. 'Now if you were a saloon keeper and young Tom was a paying customer you would not let him be needlessly gunned down. You'd keep order, Mr Noah. That's what you'd do.'

'Excuse me, Mrs Brannigan. I need a private word with Miz Polly.' Taking Polly's arm he steered her away out of earshot.

'We're city folk, Miz Polly, you and me, folk from the worst side of town. I ain't up to much when it comes to riding a horse. How the hell can I find my way to the Glover spread and back again? Furthermore, it ain't my way to go looking for trouble. I wait for it to come to my door!'

She nodded. 'Well, it has come to your door in a manner of speaking, Mr Noah. But what you say is true. You won't be able to get there alone without getting lost. I'll see to it that Clem Sawyer drives you there and back. I'll go fetch him.'

'But–'

'We're acquainted. In a manner of speaking! He's been hanging round this laundry taking every opportunity to wish me good day.'

'Lucky for you he wasn't hanging around the laundry yesterday night,' Noah muttered.

'Now that's enough of that kind of talk, Mr Noah. Stay put. I'll go fetch him.'

Noah scowled. Was it too much to hope that the useless lawman would tell her to get lost? 'Well ma'am,' he turned to Mrs Brannigan, 'if the the sheriff agrees to ride along I'll look into the matter.'

Clem Sawyer tried to argue. 'There's important work to be done in town, Miz Polly. There's a deranged lunatic at large in my town, ma'am. What kind of man practically takes off another man's head, Miz Polly?' The lawman shook his head.

'I can't answer that, Sheriff, but Mr Noah needs your help. Mr Noah is still breathing. Edgar Smith ain't, so I reckon you can leave the others searching the town for evidence whilst you head out with Mr Noah.' She smiled. 'I'd be mighty displeased if you refused to go.'

'Hell, Miz Polly, I don't know why you are concerning yourself in this matter.' He hesitated, 'I'll ride along just to please you. Now, how about a kiss before I go?'

She gave him a kiss. 'So you are attracted to me, are you, Sheriff? Why is that?'

'I can't say, Miz Polly. I guess it's your fearsome temper!'

'I'll see you when you get back.' He'd unsettled her. Maybe Clem Sawyer was smarter that she'd given him credit for.

Noah climbed into the buggy beside Clem Sawyer. 'Barkeepers are easy enough to replace. Theodore Black won't lose any sleep over Smith's demise,' the lawman ruminated.

Noah shrugged. What was there to say? He guessed Flannigan would have replaced him quickly enough.

'Same goes for schoolteachers,' Sawyer continued. 'But lawmen, they're a different breed.'

Noah knew he had to do his damnedest to keep Sawyer alive should trouble erupt at the Glover spread. With Sawyer dead he wouldn't be able to find his goddamn way back to town. The rocking of the buggy over rough ground was unsettling. The shrub-dotted landscape seemed to have no distinguishing features but nevertheless Sawyer seemed to know where he was headed.

'So tell me about the Glovers.'

Sawyer shrugged. 'They ain't none too bright although young Dotty seemed smart enough. Seth Glover now is a vicious varmint. I've seen him take a quirt to a horse.'

'So he'd be capable of taking a shot at us if riled!' Noah essayed.

'Hell, he sure is capable of squeezing a trigger if riled,' Sawyer replied without hesitation. 'His boys are big and mean. They're men who are quick to use their fists and boots when a disagreement needs to be settled.' The lawman thought for a moment. 'Say, why is Miz Polly interested in this matter?'

'Damned if I know,' Noah answered, thinking that maybe she just wanted to rile him.

'She's a caring woman, Mr Noah, a caring woman.'

'Pity she ain't a man,' Noah replied. 'She could have buckled on her guns and gone out and seen to this matter herself.' He fell silent before giving a chuckle; with Miz Polly's short fuse the Glovers might all have found themselves blasted without warning. 'Just joshing,' he responded when confronted with a look of incomprehension from Sawyer.

'Rider headed our way.' Sawyer brought the buggy to a halt.

'Is it one of the Glovers?'

'Hell no. This man is a stranger. But there shouldn't be any trouble with me being a lawman. He's seen the star and he's keeping his hands on the saddle horn.'

The man was of middling years, Noah saw, with a hard look about him. 'You reach for that shotgun and you'll be dead before you can level it,' the stranger said without preamble as he drew level with the buggy.

Noah didn't react. He didn't agree but as yet there was no need to prove the overconfident varmint wrong.

'There's no need for that tone, stranger.' The sheriff spoke mildly. 'I'm Sheriff Sawyer from Hawk's Head and this is Mr Noah, our schoolteacher. And who might you be?'

'Jericho,' the other replied. 'I'm headed for Hawk's Head. You don't object?'

'The gunman. I've heard of you.' The sheriff nodded. 'I'll see you in town. Good day to you, Mr Jericho.' He clicked the reins.

Jericho watched as the buggy moved away.

84

On a hunch he decided to follow. At a distance!

'Jericho,' Sawyer muttered. 'He's a killer for hire, that one. Could be he's here at Theodore Black's invitation. Maybe you should be worried, Mr Noah!'

Noah shrugged. Sawyer couldn't know that his only worry at the moment was getting back to Hawk's Head. Hell. He was dependent on Sawyer and didn't like the feeling. Under his breath he cussed Miz Polly for putting him in this situation. He also cussed Mrs Brannigan and her son Tom. He had a hunch he was riding into trouble. Trouble had dogged him ever since he had set foot in Hawk's Head.

'Hell!' Sawyer declared as they crested a low ridge, 'I'm a fool for letting Miz Polly persuade me to go along with this foolishness. Dotty Glover ain't our concern, Mr Noah. We don't need to pursue this matter with excessive zeal! Do you understand what I'm saying!'

'I sure do, Sheriff. But it ain't my way to lie. And I am pretty sure those two women will question us closely.'

'You have a way of riling folk, Mr Noah. Glover is a mean-hearted varmint. Leave the talking to me.' Sawyer stifled a yawn. It was just his luck to be stuck with an honest man who would not take the easy path.

Seth Glover watched the buggy approach. He was surprised to see Sawyer, the rotund lawman. His companion, the broad-shouldered galoot with cropped hair and a mean look about him he did not know.

'What brings you here, Sheriff?' he demanded as the buggy came near.

'Sure is a hot day,' the sheriff declared. 'A glass of Mrs Glover's lemonade would be much appreciated.'

'Rube, go get the sheriff a glass of lemonade,' Glover ordered.

Noah was glad he had not been included. It would not have seemed right taking a glass of lemonade from a man he might have to kill.

'Much appreciated.'

Noah saw that the sheriff had now plastered a foolish grin on his face. The grin conveyed that he was everyone's friend and that Glover had nothing to worry about.

'Thank you kindly.' Sawyer took the lemonade and gulped it down. 'I sure am parched.'

'What brings you here?' Glover was not prepared to engage in idle chatter.

'Well, Mr Noah, our new schoolteacher,

has been wondering why Dotty hasn't turned up at school,' Sawyer rejoined casually.

Something about Glover's demeanour changed. Noah noticed it. But the lawman seemed unaware of it.

There was a lengthy silence before Glover replied. 'The fact is, Sheriff, Dotty has gone, upped and run off some time ago.' He grinned. 'Seems she took exception to doing her chores.'

Sawyer nodded. 'That's fair enough. These things happen. We'll be heading back to town.'

Noah realized that the sheriff didn't give a damn about Dotty Glover. Noah didn't particularly care about young Dotty Glover either but he could not let this be. Instinct told him the girl's father was lying.

'My hunch is that Dotty could well be dead,' he drawled, hoping his words would provoke some kind of reaction.

'Dotty fell!' young Rube cried. 'It was an accident. She hit her head.'

Seth glared at Rube. Then he nodded. 'That's the truth of it. She's buried out back. As Rube says, it was a tragic accident. There ain't been no crime committed here, Sheriff.'

Sawyer nodded. 'Maybe that's so and maybe it's not. But there's no way I can get to the bottom of this matter so I guess I must take your word. You should have let me know when the accident happened. It would have saved me and Mr Noah a ride out here.'

'All the family will tell you it was an accident.' Glover insisted. 'I'm damn sorry I did not inform you, Sheriff. No offence was intended.'

'Are you satisfied, Mr Noah?' Sawyer asked without expecting a negative answer.

'No,' Noah replied bluntly. 'There's more to this than has been told. We need to take a look at the body.'

'What the hell are you talking about?' Glover demanded. 'Are you loco!'

'We're digging her up,' Noah stated flatly. 'I want to make sure she is dead and buried. If we get a look at her maybe we'll see just how she died. For all we know you folk may have hogtied her and buried her alive.'

'You're mad,' Glover yelled.

'So I've been told. But we are not leaving here until we know the truth.'

CHAPTER 6

'You're insane!' Seth Glover declared. 'Mr Noah, you belong in an asylum! No decent-minded man would ask that a young girl's body be dug up just to satisfy idle curiosity. This isn't decent. What do you say, Sheriff? Can't you make this lunatic see sense!'

'Now, Mr Noah, I am sure this ain't necessary.' Sawyer looked decidedly unhappy.

'Well it damn well is. We're here to find the truth. We've heard two different stories: first she ran off, second she fell and hit her head. I'm not convinced that we've heard the truth!'

'So where is she buried?' Sawyer asked. 'Show us the marker and we'll be satisfied.'

The silence lengthened. A muscle beneath Seth Glover's eye twitched.

'Fact is there ain't no marker,' Rube bleated. His three elder brothers had joined him on the porch.

'That don't seem right,' the sheriff rejoined.

'Get the hell off my property,' Seth Glover bawled. 'Get the hell off my property or I won't be responsible!'

In an instant Noah had levelled his rifle.

'Don't none of you even twitch,' he warned. 'I'm liable to take off someone's head if I feel nervous and twitching makes me mighty nervous. Now, Sheriff, you get down out of this buggy. Get inside and search the house.' He paused. 'If anyone makes a move young Rube will be the first to get his head blown off.'

'You murderous lunatic,' Glover grated furiously. 'You'll pay for this. Mark my words, you're gonna pay.'

Grim-faced Sawyer climbed down from the buggy. 'Hell, Mr Noah, this is a damn waste of time. We're making fools of ourselves.'

'Just get in there and search the house. And do a good job. Can you at least do that?'

The muscle beneath Glover's eye continued to twitch. One of his sons had started to sweat. Another shifted uncomfortably. Noah wondered whether he would indeed take off Rube's head should trouble erupt. He didn't know. He'd never seen himself as a cold-blooded killer. But something was mighty wrong and he aimed to get to the bottom of things.

Time seemed to pass slowly whilst Sawyer searched. No one spoke. Mindful of the lunatic schoolteacher, Seth Glover did not even dare bat away a fly that landed on his nose.

'Goddamn you, Mr Noah. Goddamn you!' he muttered threateningly.

'Well, she ain't inside.' Sawyer said as he emerged from the house.

Noah stared hard at the lawman. A faded-looking woman, clearly Mrs Glover, followed Sawyer from the house. She gave a toothless smile. 'Would *you* care for a glass of lemonade before you leave, Mr Noah!'

'Hell!' Noah yelled. 'You no account two-bit tin star, you've been sitting in there supping lemonade! Ain't I right! Get back in there and get your head into every damn cupboard after you've poked your snout into the cellar. You goddamn useless pig!'

Clem Sawyer did not reply. It was Glover who reacted. With a roar of rage the man lowered his head and charged towards Noah.

Noah shot him in the leg and Glover went down with a pained yell.

'Stay put,' Noah bellowed at the four Glover boys.

'Hell, Mr Noah, we must stop the blood before he bleeds to death,' Clem Sawyer said, springing at last into action.

'Get on with it.' Noah kept the others covered.

'She's in the cellar,' Rube blubbed.

'Shut your goddamn mouth, Rube,' his brothers yelled with such ferocity that Noah knew Rube had spoken the truth, although whether she was alive or dead in the cellar remained to be discovered. He watched as Seth's wound was tightly bound.

'I'll look in the cellar.' Sawyer wiped his brow. He clearly wanted this business over with.

'No!' Mrs Glover screamed, throwing herself at the lawman. She hung on to his arm, refusing to let go. And then she made the mistake of trying to grab his .45. Sawyer cursing, struck out at the woman, shoving her away from him with considerable force. Screaming, she collapsed in the dirt and covered her head with her apron.

Sawyer cussed and hurried into the house. When he emerged it was with a filth-begrimed figure wrapped in a stinking blanket. 'Dotty Glover,' he declared. 'The varmints have been keeping her locked in the cellar. Hell, who would have thought...' He paused. 'Leastways she ain't dead.'

'She shamed the family, shamed the family,' Mrs Glover screamed.

'Get your pa and sister into the buggy,' Noah ordered the four Glover boys. 'And you, Sawyer, get back inside that house. Gather up every damn weapon you can find. I'm not having them taking chance shots as we ride out.'

'He ought to have strangled her,' Mrs Glover cried. 'But no, that would be murder, he said. So he put her in the cellar and prayed that natural causes would take her. And now he's crippled because of her and you, Mr Noah. May the devil take you as well.'

Sawyer stuffed the weaponry he had collected into a sack. 'Don't worry, Mr Noah. I ain't overlooked a single shooter. Now I'll just turn their horses loose and then we can be away. We're hightailing it out of here, Mr Noah, pretty damn quick I can tell you. Why, I just don't trust myself around this loco bunch.'

Noah eyed the Glovers. 'Let this be an end to it!' he told them. 'It's the best way. Your pa will pull through. You have a farm to tend!' He climbed aboard the buggy.

Jericho had watched the scene below unfold with interest. Whistling, he turned away and headed for Hawk's Head. Taking a shorter route not suited to wheels, he arrived in town some time before the buggy.

'Hell, Mr Noah, what are we going to do

with Dotty Glover?' Sawycr asked as they drove into town. 'There ain't no one going to want to take care of her considering her condition.'

'As to that,' Noah rejoined, 'why, didn't you say Miz Polly has a kind heart?'

Sawyer did not reply. But he brought the buggy to a halt in front of the laundry. Miz Polly and Mrs Brannigan, alerted by the commotion, came out. Folk crowded around the buggy where Dotty Glover, very pregnant by the look of her, cowered beneath her blanket. She was not getting a sympathetic reception. The sympathy was being directed at her pa, who was being driven over to the doc's place.

'Shame on you, Mr Noah. You ought not to have meddled. You should have known better. A good man's been shot,' someone yelled.

'Get her inside, Miz Polly,' Noah said, 'and don't you say a word about it was you and Mrs Brannigan that sent me out looking for Dotty. Well, here she is and I reckon it falls to you, Miz Polly, to look after her. That should teach you not to meddle.'

Pastor Webb appeared outside the laundry. He held up a conciliatory hand. 'What's done is done. We'll get the asylum wagon for

Dotty Glover.' Murmurs of assent greeted his words. 'Dotty Glover has shamed her family,' he continued. 'The town is well rid of her.'

'No!' Noah's voice was loud. 'We're not sending for any damn cart. I'll deal with anyone who thinks different.'

'But she's clearly deranged!'

'You sanctimonious meddler.' Noah shoved the pastor, sending him staggering back into the arms of his sister. Both fell to the floor and Noah could not help but observe that Miss Agatha Webb had a mighty trim ankle.

'You're a ruffian, Mr Noah. How dare you!' She scrambled to her feet.

The laundry door slammed shut. CLOSED, said a notice that appeared at the window.

'Goddamnit, Mr Noah!' an irate *hombre* yelled, 'Thanks to your meddling I ain't able to get my dudes washed today.'

'You are a brute, Mr Noah,' Agatha Webb cried. 'I'll pray for you.'

'You're not fit to teach this town's children!' her brother accused.

'My boy is coming along real well,' a farmer spoke up. 'You're doing a fine job, Mr Noah, and that's a fact.'

'Why, thank you.' Noah, turning, saw that Theodore Black had joined the crowd. Also lounging on the edge of the crowd was the gunman he and the sheriff had encountered earlier. The man looked amused by the ruckus that had erupted.

Something had changed in this town, Black realized. Things had started to change the day that damn interfering polecat Mr Noah had stepped down from the train. Folk were ignoring the rancher. It was the schoolteacher who was the centre of attention.

'What the hell is going on?' the rancher bellowed. 'I want to know who killed my man Edgar Smith!'

'Well, as to that, we cannot say.' Clem Sawyer had returned. 'The town has been searched for incriminating evidence. Nothing has been found. I'd say it was a vagrant heading through town. Smith's pockets had been emptied of cash.' The lawman shrugged, 'It won't be hard for you to find another bartender, Mr Black. A man like Smith won't be missed.'

'You're a disgrace to your badge,' Black spat angrily.

'Am I?' the lawman yelled. 'Well next time you're thinking of lynching a widelooper maybe you had better bring him in for trial.

Things have been too darn lax around here. Times are changing, Mr Black. And keep an eye on that no-account son of yours. I've had a bellyful of trouble being stirred up in my town.'

The two men glared at one another. And then the rancher turned away, aware that in possessing the star Sawyer had the advantage. He had the law on his side.

Theodore Black decided to swing by the Glover place on his way home. He'd have a word with Glover's none too bright boys. They could be used, used to eliminate Mr Noah. By God, that man had got too big for his damn boots.

Mrs Glover felt as though she had been caught up in a maelstrom. The lives of the Glovers had been wrecked. If Seth didn't heal well the work needing to be done to keep the place going was bound to suffer. He'd always kept the boys in line with the implied threat of violence towards anyone fool enough to argue with him. If only he had listened to her this would not have happened. She'd told him to finish Dotty off. But he'd elected to imprison Dotty in the cellar. There'd been no reasoning with him and now he'd been shot. And the boys were at the whiskey bottle, swearing revenge on Mr Noah and Clem Sawyer. They were also yelling out for her to get them something to eat.

'We've been shamed,' she screamed. 'Shamed in the eyes of the town and all you can think about is filling your bellies.'

An empty bottle shattered against the wall beside her head. 'Shut up, Ma, and rustle up some grub,' Rube yelled.

Knowing plenty about human nature Noah knew the Glover boys would be bearing a grudge. He tried to put himself in their boots. They'd get liquored up, that was for sure, and then what would they do?

The school building was situated on the outskirts of town, presumably to put distance between the youngsters and any ruckus that might arise on Main Street. But it also meant that there was distance between the town and any trouble that came knocking on the schoolhouse door. Presumably the luckless Edward White had been dragged from the schoolhouse, taken out of town and then tarred and feathered. And no one had seen a damn thing!

Sawyer could not be counted upon to be of any use. Noah guessed he was alone. But then he had never needed a helping hand when it had come to dealing with trouble.

He cooked his evening meal. He then cleared up and washed his dishes. He took up his shotgun and prepared himself for the night ahead. He'd thought things through and had decided that anyone who came gunning for him did not deserve a chance to come back another day to finish the job. He hoped they wouldn't come. It had hit him hard today, the fact that he'd grown tired of violence. Hell, what he wanted, he realized with surprise, was a quiet life, the same as other folk. But hell, a quiet life seemed destined to elude him in this two-bit town. Straightening his shoulders he left the schoolhouse.

In Black's Saloon Jericho was enjoying a beer. He listened to the gossip around him. Mostly it concerned the schoolteacher and how he'd got away with crippling Seth Glover. Men were saying Mr Noah was a meddling no-good and that Dotty Glover had got what was coming to her.

'Let's hope she drowns herself in one of those goddamn laundry tubs!' a galoot declared and loud guffaws ensued.

Jericho did not join the laughter. He finished his beer and returned to the hotel.

He set his chair by the window and took up his vigil. He had a hunch that the night coming was not going to be an uneventful one!

If the Glovers came they'd come in from the north, Noah decided. They would not want to attract attention to themselves by riding through town. Noah settled down behind a massive felled tree that was reasonably near to the schoolhouse. He could have told Mrs Brannigan to let things be, but he'd known damn well she wouldn't have listened, likewise Miz Polly. And he had seen it in their eyes when he'd told the Glovers to let the matter be, that his words had fallen on deaf ears.

'So why ain't the high and mighty Mr Theodore Black riding with you?' Mrs Glover demanded. She glared at her sons.

'Hell, Ma, like Theodore said, it's our pa who has been gunned. We're the ones who have got to deal out justice. Like Theodore said, he won't be expecting us. He thinks he has got away with it. And damn Clem Sawyer ain't going to bother about another dead schoolteacher. Once Theodore makes it known Noah has got his just deserts no one in Hawk's Head is going to give a damn.'

Young Rube Glover gulped down what was left of his whiskey. 'Let's ride. Let's send that varmint to hell where he belongs.'

'Black's using you! He don't give a damn about your pa,' Mrs Glover yelled. 'And you're too damn stupid to see it. And that varmint will be expecting you!'

'Just get out of the way, Ma!' Simon, Rube's eldest brother, gave her a shove. 'Mr Noah is gonna burn. He's going to hell where he belongs. This is man's work! We're gonna torch that schoolhouse. That varmint is going to burn in his bed. And then he's headed for hell!'

Noah felt the rough-textured bark against his back. Every now and then his head would fall forward and his eyes would begin to close. Keeping watch was not his forte. Nor was teaching school. Sliding drinks along a bar, listening to idle chatter, watching out to see who was going to take one drink too many, who was going to erupt with the intention of causing trouble and damage, that was his life. Goddamn it, frontier life was not for him. He was missing the East. When this was over he was headed home.

He heard them coming, the muffled sounds of horses, an almighty belch from one of the riders, a muffled curse, and there was something else, the smell of kerosene. The varmints intended to burn him whilst he slept. Well, by bringing that goddamn kerosene along they had played into his hands. He wouldn't show them any mercy. Men wanting to torch another did not deserve mercy.

Horses, dark shadows in the night, passed by his place of concealment. All four of the Glovers were in on this. He could hear their excited whispering. He felt a great calmness descend on him. He was not afraid. He felt detached from all of this.

They dismounted before the darkened schoolhouse. The smell of the kerosene intensified as they sloshed it over the dry wood of the building. These men were taking the coward's way. These would be no open challenge, no calls for him to come on out and answer for what he'd done to their pa. They came like thieves in the night, determined upon murder.

'Get back. Hell, we don't want to torch ourselves,' one of them hissed a warning to the others. Noah found himself hoping that the fools *would* accidentally torch themselves. He readied himself. He needed to hit his targets first time round. He couldn't afford to make the mistake of missing a target. That was all they were to him now, targets within range of his rifle.

In the darkness a match was struck and dropped into the kerosene. A thread of flame raced towards the schoolhouse. The fire took hold, increasing in intensity, lighting the area directly before the burning schoolhouse door.

The Glovers yelled and whooped, clearly hoping to see a burning schoolteacher staggering from the flames demented with pain, dying on his feet.

'Don't no one put him out of his misery,' one of them bellowed.

Coming up on to one knee, unseen in the darkness Noah sighted on his clearly visible capering targets. Taking aim he fired.

A bullet thudded into the back of Rube's head. He died before he'd realized what was happening. His three surviving brothers went down like skittles beneath Noah's rapid and deadly fire. There were screams, then silence, unbroken except for the crackling of the flames.

He wiped his brow. Now that it was over townsfolk were running towards the schoolhouse. He smiled grimly. He could not see a bucket between them, not that a few pails of water could stop this fire. The schoolhouse and the school were done for. And so was he. He'd had a bellyful of Hawk's Head. He was heading for somewhere civilized.

Jericho heard the shooting and saw the flames from his hotel room. His bet was on the schoolteacher, a man who was suited to many things other than teaching school. He shook his head. Those fool farmers had thought themselves able to dispatch a man to whom killing came natural. Putting on his hat he went to see if he'd guessed correctly how this matter had turned out. On Main Street he saw a sight that stopped him in his tracks.

The farmer, Seth Glover, crutch under his arm, had staggered out of the doc's place. A bandage was unpeeling itself from his leg as Glover's face contorted with pain. Then with a hoarse cry, Glover fell to the ground. The man tried to lever himself to his feet but failed. He began to bleed profusely as his life ebbed away.

Townsfolk were running about like demented ants. No one had noticed Glover. Not yet. Jericho guessed that the wound had started bleeding again. Glover needed help.

Callously the gunman ignored him. He strolled on towards the burning schoolhouse. When he saw the four dead men positioned by townsfolk in a neat row Jericho was not surprised. Noah had dealt with his enemies in the same way that Jericho himself would have done.

CHAPTER 7

Noah checked into the hotel. The schoolhouse had been burnt to a cinder and the five Glover men were laid out at the undertakers. Significantly no one had congratulated him on his escape from death.

'The devil looks after his own,' a waddy declared. 'And he is as sure as hell looking after you, Mr Noah.' There was a note of condemnation in the voice that Noah did not much care for. He ignored the fool.

There were a few days to pass until the eastbound train came through. He aimed to be on it.

'Seems like you're out of a job, Mr Noah,' the hotel clerk observed slyly. 'Now what are you going to do. You're going to have a hell of a job to get this town to honour your contract and pay your wages.'

'I'm headed out,' Noah rejoined. 'And

you're going to have a hell of a job getting this town to pay my rooming charge for these last few days.' He winked. 'Looks like we're both going to have one hell of a job!'

'And you've done one hell of a good job tonight Mr Noah, if I may say so.'

Noah nodded at the gunman.

'My name's Jericho,' the man introduced himself.

'So, have we got anything to settle?' For one moment he wondered whether that snake Theodore Black had hired this gunman to kill him.

'Nope. I'm here on a personal matter,' the other rejoined, realizing the drift of Noah's thoughts.

Noah nodded. 'See you around.'

'Maybe.' Jericho likewise nodded.

'And to think I believed you to be a God-fearing churchgoing man,' Miss Agatha Webb hissed as she spotted Noah heading for the station. 'This town is better off without you! You are an unworthy man, no better than a hired killer.' She took a deep breath. 'If you're going to shoot me for speaking the truth, Mr Noah, I have no regrets.'

He wasn't going to let her get away with this and knew just how to send her fleeing.

'Well, Miss Agatha,' he drawled, 'there are plenty of things I'd like to do to you but killing you ain't one of them.'

'How dare you!'

'I'd dare plenty if you just give me the word, Miss Agatha.' He was enjoying this. He grinned. And watched as Miss Agatha, picking up her skirts, swiftly departed.

A commotion occurred across Main Street. Tom Brannigan, his face as red as his hair, came tumbling out of the laundry door. Miz Polly, bucket in hand, appeared at the door and promptly threw the contents of the bucket over young Tom. 'Get out of here and don't come back,' she yelled. Then, catching sight of Noah, shouted angrily, 'And just what are you looking at, Mr Noah?'

He ignored the troublesome woman. Whistling cheerfully he continued on his way. Theodore Black, he observed, was lounging against the hitching rail. There was an odd expression on the rancher's face. Catching Noah's eye the man quickly looked away.

'You've brought nothing but grief to this town, Mr Noah.' Pastor Webb fell into step beside him. 'The widow Glover has hung herself and you are to blame!'

'I don't give a damn about the widow Glover. And the way I see things, this town has done nothing but cause me grief. Truth is, I am glad to shake the dust of Hawk's Head off my boots. Now get out of my sight, you damn sanctimonious fool, before I forget you are wearing a dog collar.'

The train was ready and waiting. It was a welcome sight. He climbed aboard and settled down with a sigh of contentment. He was free at last of this damn two-bit town.

Inside the laundry Polly heard the whistle of the departing train. She'd been rushed off her feet looking after Dolly Glover and having to cope with the laundry work. Dolly Glover was tough. She reminded Polly of a younger version of herself. What Dolly had gone through would have driven a lesser woman mad. But Dolly was a survivor and...

'Well, he's gone.' The ostler staggered in with a sack of dudes stinking of the stable.

'Who's gone?'

'Mr Noah. He's headed back East.'

'Hell!' Noah was a varmint but she'd known he would come to her aid if needs be. Alone in a frontier town she needed someone on her side. And the only someone she could think of now was Clem Sawyer, the town's useless lawman. She'd heard he had not been such a bum in his younger days, before he'd piled on weight. Whether that was true or not

Sawyer wore a badge and that counted for something. There was no alternative, she must mosey over and see Clem Sawyer.

Clem Sawyer nearly fell off his chair with shock when Miz Polly sauntered in and put her booted foot on his desk. She had a mighty fine leg, he noticed.

'I never got round to thanking you, Sheriff Sawyer,' she told him softly. 'There ain't no time like the present, I say.'

'Well, I ain't a man to turn a lady away,' Sawyer croaked, unable to believe his good luck.

Theodore Black headed for his saloon. He paused as he reached the lounging gunman.

'Are you looking for work, stranger? I can always use a top gun.'

'Nope,' Jericho answered flatly.

'I'll keep the offer open.' Theodore offered generously.

Jericho didn't reply. The Brannigan boy, he saw, had sneaked into the laundry whilst the red-haired harridan running the show had disappeared into the sheriff's office. She'd been in there a mighty long time, Jericho reflected, as he headed for the laundry. The place smelt of damp clothes and steam.

'I want to see Dotty!' the boy was saying, 'Just to see if she's all right.'

The small Chinese woman tried to push him out.

'Excuse me.' A woman practically shoved Jericho from the doorway. Mrs Brannigan marched into the laundry.

Surreptitiously Jericho studied the woman who was his sister. They'd been parted as youngsters when their folk had died, each farmed out with different folk. He'd tracked her down simply because he'd felt curious. Well here she was, his sister and his nephew both getting hot under the collar and it wasn't because of the steam.

A stone crashed through the window.

'Dotty Glover; you get out of our town,' voices yelled. 'You ain't wanted.'

'You're wearing a gun!' Mrs Brannigan grabbed her son's arm. 'You ain't going out there.'

'I'm gonna protect Dotty. There ain't no one running her out of town.'

'Give me that gun! I'll deal with this, Tom,' Mrs Brannigan shouted, grabbing hold of her son's arm.

'I'll deal with the matter!' Jericho declared. His damn fool sister was indeed intending to confront the angry crowd gathered outside.

'They wouldn't be here if Mr Noah hadn't left town,' Tom told his ma. Jericho hardly heard the boy. He was on his way out to deal with the troublemakers outside.

'Get about your business.' Jericho faced the crowd. He noticed that a good many respectable women were there, egging on their men. The pastor was also there, stirring up trouble. 'I'm making this my concern,' Jericho told them. 'And I am telling the lot of you to leave the Glover girl in peace.'

'What's this got to do with you?'

'Why, I am a galoot who wants his dudes washed, and with all this commotion and upheaval getting my dudes washed don't seem likely. Now get out of here, you polecats and leave this laundry and its womenfolk be.'

'You are right, this is not your concern.' The pastor was not going to back down. 'This is a decent town with God-fearing men and women and—'

Jericho hauled iron. 'Another word and you'll be missing part of your foot. I ain't got time for sanctimonious fools. Go on! Get out of here. If anyone wants to argue we will settle the matter in the time-honoured way: fastest man with the Peacemaker calls the shots.'

'In this case the law calls the shots.' The sheriff had appeared at last. 'And I am inclined to agree with the stranger. You folk are to leave this laundry be and the women-folk as well.' He glared at the crowd. 'Those Glovers brought misfortune upon themselves. And that is an end of the matter. Young Dotty has as much right to walk down Main Street as the rest of you. Savvy!'

'Have you gone mad, Sheriff?' the pastor cried.

'Another word out of you and I'll gut you like a fish,' Jericho snarled, losing patience.

'Just get out of here,' the sheriff insisted. 'Not you, Pastor Webb! A night in a flea-infested cell ought to curb your enthusiasm for meddling. Get moving. Head for the jail. Don't make me drag you there!'

'Now listen, Sheriff.' A farmer squared up to the lawman. He didn't get very far. Sawyer's clenched fist rammed into the man's stomach, causing him to double over. Sawyer's other fist connected with the farmer's head. He sank to his knees.

There was a stunned silence. No one in this town had ever seen this side of Clem Sawyer, at least not for a mighty long while.

'You'll answer to your Maker for this, Sheriff Sawyer.' Pastor Webb summoned up what dignity he could muster and began to walk towards the jail.

Men began to disperse. Clem Sawyer

didn't trouble himself speaking to the gunman who'd chosen to intervene in this little fracas.

Miz Polly, swinging her hips, sauntered into the laundry. 'There ain't nothing to fret about, Mrs Brannigan. Sheriff Sawyer – well, he'll be siding with us from now on. I'll make sure of it.'

'But where is Mr Noah?' Mrs Brannigan asked.

'Why he's left town, Mrs Brannigan. He's headed East, which is where he and I hail from. I didn't know his plans until after he left. I've not had time to set foot out of this laundry since Dotty Glover arrived.'

'But he can't leave. Tom is doing real well and it's all on account of Mr Noah's teaching! Why, if I had known about this I would have stopped him, Miss Polly.'

'I'd have stopped him myself had I realized you wanted him to stay around, Mrs Brannigan. But how could I know?' She realized that the gunman was gawking at them. 'Where's your laundry?' she snapped.

'I'm just checking out your prices,' Jericho told her. Did they really think they would have been able to stop Mr Noah leaving town, a man who had just recently killed all four of the Glover boys with an efficiency

Jericho had to admire. The schoolteacher had escaped just in time. His sister and Miz Polly didn't sound right in the head!

'Clear as day!' She pointed to the tariff on the wall. 'Now you've checked them you ain't got cause to hang around.'

'Good day to you, sir.' Mrs Brannigan glared at him. Jericho retreated. He had been expecting to be thanked, maybe even tearfully thanked, but thanks, he saw, were not forthcoming. He guessed he didn't blame Noah for leaving town. At least the man's troubles were over. He'd make himself known to his sister later, a widow who was doing her damnedest to keep her farm afloat.

'Maybe young Tom has had something to do with Dotty's condition,' he quipped.

'How dare you!' His enraged sister snatched up a pail of water and threw it over him. Jericho retreated. Now was not the time to make their relationship known.

Agatha Webb found herself obliged to wait until Theodore Black, who was drinking at his saloon, came out.

'Mr Black!' She hurried after him.

Theodore Black had as little contact as possible with respectable women such as Agatha Webb. He'd been obliged to marry one after all, young Freddy's ma, who'd done nothing but nag him until the day she had died. As Miss Webb was now blocking his path he was obliged to stop and listen whilst she gabbled on about Pastor Webb and how he was now suffering the indignity of being locked in a cell.

'Surely you can speak to Sheriff Sawyer, make him see reason, make him release my brother! Please help us, Mr Black.'

He touched his hat, a token of respect. 'I have not got time to waste on such nonsense, Miss Webb. I am a busy man. I have matters to attend to, matters of great importance. Now if you will excuse me.'

Agatha Webb made the mistake of grabbing his arm. 'You can't walk away. You must understand...'

His large hand closed over her small hand. Theodore Black gave her hand a squeeze, enough to hurt her. 'As I've said, Miss Webb, I am a busy man. Please excuse me. Remove your hand from my arm.' He squeezed again. Agatha Webb almost screamed with pain. But she'd been raised to be dignified at all times. She removed her hand from his arm. 'I see that we understand each other, Miss Webb. Please don't bother me with this kind of nonsense again.

Pastor Webb jumped in without testing the water, as they say. To my way of thinking he is lucky the gunman didn't take off the top of his head. That kind of low-down vermin just looks for an excuse to kill. Why, sometimes they don't need an excuse.' He took a step away from her. 'I can't figure out why that killer wanted to involve himself in such foolishness. Good day to you, Miss Webb. And just you remember, any man fool enough to grab hold of my arm, I'd see to it he wouldn't be able to walk away. Lucky for you that you are a fool of a female.'

He strode away leaving her standing there, mouth open, frozen with shock. He'd told her the goddamn truth. He did indeed have important matters to attend to. He was a man who seized opportunity when it came along. When the Glover boys had burnt down the schoolhouse it had been too bad that Noah had been expecting them. That Noah would blast all four of them was an eventuality that he had not anticipated. But he had anticipated that with the schoolhouse a charred ruin and townspeople muttering that Mr Noah was a no-account meddling killer, the schoolteacher would have had a bellyful of Hawk's Head and thus decide to leave town. The hotel clerk had been more than happy to confirm that Noah was going.

Theodore could not forget how he'd been obliged to back down by Noah, obliged to let that murderously inclined little varmint, the Dobbs boy, keep on breathing. And then young Freddy had been thrown in a cell with three rotting carcasses. Why, Mr Noah obliged me to do it, Sawyer had bleated, adding that some might say young Freddy was damn fortunate to be breathing as he'd been fool enough to hire killers not up to the job.

'You ain't going to let him get away with what he's done to me, are you, Pa?' Freddy kept whimpering, and Theodore had assured his son that Mr Noah would indeed be put in his place.

Theodore smiled savagely; that fool of a schoolteacher believed he was leaving trouble behind him but truth was he was heading towards it. Now all that was needed was to collect young Freddy and some of the crew and they'd have themselves some fun at Mr Noah's expense.

The men he chose would ride with him without a qualm. He'd offer them a bonus, assure them that they were just going to have themselves some fun teaching a jumped-up varmint who'd killed four of the town's men, the Glovers, without batting an eyelid and then, just to make sure it was an offer they couldn't refuse, he'd offer free drinks all round for those who rode with him.

Noah leant back against the upholstery. It smelt of the countless cigars that had been smoked on this train. Miz Polly seemed to have landed on her feet, he reflected: seems like she'd quit drinking and had taken over the running of the laundry. Naturally enough those damn fools in Hawk's Head hadn't realized just what she was capable of when riled. Hell, he could not understand why Clem Sawyer was smitten with that woman. But that was not his concern. Hawk's Head was behind him, he could forget about the town and its folk.

'Coffee, sir?' The enquirer was not Tubbs.

'Where's Tubbs?'

The man smiled. 'Well, you know Tubbs. He's laid low, it seems he got into a ruckus with a hobo riding for free. He's on the mend. But don't you be forgetting, sir, the railway has more than one conductor! Me now, I would have let that hobo be. There ain't no cause to go looking for trouble, I say.'

Noah nodded. He was not surprised. Tubbs was a pugnacious galoot. This *hombre* seemed the exact opposite to Tubbs, tall and lanky with a gangling appearance that did not suggest any forcefulness of character.

'I'll take a coffee.'

'Last of the pot, sir.' The man poured a cupful and it looked strong enough to dissolve the lining of a man's stomach. Just how Noah liked his coffee. 'You can have it for free seeing as how it's just the dregs of the pot.'

'Suits me.' Noah sipped his coffee. He closed his eyes. He was safe on board a train. He could relax until he reached his destination. When those fool Glovers had attacked the schoolhouse they'd done him a favour. He'd been given the incentive he needed to quit town. His eyelids felt heavy. He had a vague feeling of unease before he lost consciousness.

Lynch the conductor made his way forward to have a word with the driver and fireman. All three of them were in on it. Had Tubbs been around things would have been different, for Tubbs was an honest man. By a stroke of luck the big hobo had put Tubbs out of action.

The big-shot rancher had sounded out the three of them. They had all been agreeable. Theodore Black had been more than generous. Lynch had offered to do the job himself. But to his surprise Black, grabbing him by the shirt, had practically lifted him from the ground. 'You hurt one hair of that man's head and I'll peg you out to dry in the sun. You hear me! I'm calling the shots. You do what you are told and no more.'

Lynch had understood. The man had wanted more than to see Mr Noah dead. The crazy galoot was after vengeance. Lynch had known better than to ask what Mr Noah had done to rile the rancher.

It had been agreed that the train would slow to a crawl as it reached the landmark known as Needle's Point. Lynch, in preparation for the stop, hauled an insensible Mr Noah to his feet and dragged him out of the carriage. 'He's had a mite too much to drink,' he explained. But no one was interested. Sweating profusely Lynch got the insensible Mr Noah into the guard's van. He opened a door and waited.

Drunks had been known to fall from trains. No one was going to ask any questions about Mr Noah. Lynch waited as the train began to slow, too soon and the man might be done for. The train always slowed as it approached Needle's Point, so there was nothing unusual about today. Judging the train had slowed sufficiently – it was hardly moving at all – Lynch sent an unconscious Mr Noah on his way.

Rounding the bend the train began to pick up speed again. No one noticed the body lying beside the track.

CHAPTER 8

Freddy was practically crowing. 'I knew you'd make him pay for what he'd done to me, Pa!'

'You keep your mouth shut about this,' Theodore warned. 'I don't want you bragging to your no-account friends. He glowered at his son. 'I mean it. This is men's work. And men know when to keep their mouths shut.'

'You can count on me, Pa,' Freddy said. He hated that damn schoolteacher, Mr Noah.

Ruskin, one of the crew, laughed. 'Let's hope so, boy. There's law in the territory and old Clem Sawyer ain't as useless as folk might suppose.'

Theodore almost told Ruskin to shut his mouth, but Ruskin was popular with the crew and Theodore knew he needed him with them. If Ruskin went along with something then sure as hell the others would follow. And Ruskin was highly amused by what Theodore had done. 'Don't that beat all?' he had cackled more than once.

'Yep. This will be a day to remember,' Ruskin observed to no one in particular as they mounted their horses. 'Beats hard work any time. Today will be a real pleasure.'

Groaning, Noah opened his eyes. The top of his head felt as though it was going to explode. He lurched unsteadily to his feet. For a moment he was paralysed with fear. He was stranded. He stared at the expanse of track before him. Realization hit him: he'd been drugged and dumped from the train. He ought to be dead. And then as he looked towards Needle's Point he remembered that the train always slowed as it hit this particular section of track.

The damn conductor had to be responsible. He remembered drinking the bitter coffee. He stared up at the blazing sky. Was that the intention, that he should stumble around this wilderness, being driven mad with thirst, stumbling around until he collapsed and died a lonely death. His derringer and his money-belt were missing. So were his boots. Why the hell hadn't they killed him outright? They'd know that if by a miracle he survived he'd hunt them down and make them pay.

It didn't take him long to work out the obvious. They'd been paid to dump him out here alive. The boots were gone because they didn't want him getting far. Not that this was likely. Only one man could have paid that conductor. Theodore Black was behind this. The rancher imagined he had a score to settle and he was not a man to let things be.

He could not just stand here waiting for God knew what. He started towards the jutting rock that was Needle's Point cussing softly as the rocky ground hurt his bare feet. The ground was hot, it felt as though his feet were on fire. Sweat trickled down his face. He felt helpless alone out here. Reaching the jutting pillar of rock he rested his back against its hot surface. Was he mad enough to climb it, he wondered? Would it help to see the lie of the land hereabouts? Was there a farm or maybe a ranch nearby, a place he could make for and find help? Or should he just stay here by the rock waiting to see whether Theodore Black turned up. Remembering what had happened to his predecessor, the luckless Edward White, he guessed that maybe be was mad enough to try and get to the summit of the jutting rock. Hell, what did it matter if he fell and killed himself, it was better than dying of thirst or being dispatched by that no account lunatic Theodore Black and his mangy crew.

It could be done. There were nooks and crannies, jagged rocks, stunted bushes but it would be one hell of a climb and the slightest mistake would see him go down to certain death. He wasn't thinking straight. He knew that. He'd gone past the stage of listening to the voice of reason. Gritting his teeth he began to climb, pressing himself against the rock face, searching out holds for his hands and feet, praying that somehow he'd make it out of this mess alive.

He reached the top, hands and feet bleeding, legs turning to jelly, his breath escaping in laboured gasps, and all he could do was to lie there, amazed that he was still alive. Stunted scrub grew up here and the rock floor, he saw, was jagged and cracked. He staggered around his new territory, scanning the terrain set out below him, hope fading when he could not spot any signs of life; there were no smoking chimneys indicating that folk were scratching a living out here, no watering holes, although he did see a stray cow in the scrub far below.

Then he saw them, dots moving across the terrain, bunched together, riders heading for the railway tracks and the place where he'd been dumped. There was nowhere he could go! Nowhere he could run to. He squatted down, his eyes falling on a piece of jagged rock.

He settled down to wait and watch. All he could do was hope that the hunting party, when they failed to find him, would give up and head back to Theodore Black's ranch.

'Well, there ain't no sign of him!' Smithers the ramrod declared. 'But I don't reckon he will have gone far.'

'If that varmint Lynch has double-crossed me....' Theodore grated as he fought to control his rage at being cheated out of the intended sport with Mr Noah.

'Easy, boss, he's wandered away, that's all,' Ruskin cackled. 'But he ain't going to get far barefooted. These stones will cut his feet to ribbons and that's a fact.'

Theodore nodded. 'Spread out. We'll make a search. I want him alive. That presumptuous varmint needs reminding of his place.'

'You aim to kill him, then?' Smithers asked, and his boss's silence was answer enough.

'Wherever he is I'll spot him from the

Point,' Ruskin declared. 'Spotting him will earn me the bonus, won't it, boss?'

'Are you damn crazy man!' Theodore rejoined impatiently.

'Oh, it's been done. I've been up there myself a while back,' Ruskin replied. 'I went up for a wager with a galoot named Crook. You remember Crook? Stampede got him six years back.'

'If you think you can manage it, go ahead. If you spot him the bonus is yours,' Theodore told him. 'If you fall it's on your own head. You ain't been ordered to climb up!'

'No fear of that, boss.' Ruskin headed for Needle's Point.

Noah's heart lurched when he saw them headed his way. His luck had run out. He cursed. His hand tightened over the jagged rock. Cautiously he peered downwards; just one of them had dismounted. The others remained bunched together whilst the lone man began the ascent. Noah determined to go down fighting. There was nowhere to hide up here. He'd be spotted soon enough and as whoever was coming up was packing hardware it was reasonable to assume he'd be blasted on sight if he didn't act first. Acting first meant smashing in the skull of whoever hauled themselves over the edge.

126

About halfway up Ruskin began to realize that maybe he'd bitten off more than he could chew. When he'd done this climb he'd been far younger. He began to have doubts about his ability to get back down again. He struggled on, breath wheezing from his lips and he had never felt so glad as when the top of the rock was within reach. He reached over the rim, his hands closing over a stunted bush. With a sigh of relief he hauled himself over. A hand grabbed him, yanked him forward and before he had realized what was happening a rock crashed down on his skull, time and time again.

Once he'd whacked the old coot Noah found he could not stop. He was fuelled by rage. Why the hell was this man whom he had never harmed, a galoot he did not know, going along with hunting him down? He pounded away until the strength drained from his arm. Blood spattered his clothes.

From down below voices yelled. 'Any sign of that varmint, Ruskin?'

'Hell, Ruskin, this ain't no time to take a breather.'

Noah let them shout.

'Hell, I'm going up after him,' someone yelled. But whoever it was didn't get far. A yell announced that the speaker had fallen.

'Dammit, I've done twisted my ankle.'

Black ignored the fool of a waddy. He stared upwards. Realization began to dawn. Noah was up there. He had to be. And he must have killed Ruskin. The rancher had never imagined Noah capable of making such a climb.

It was an impasse, Black realized. They could not get up to get Noah and Noah could not come down whilst they were there. The rancher cursed with frustration. He couldn't get his hands on Noah. All he could do was make sure the man died from starvation and thirst. Noah would go slowly mad up there while he was waiting to die. Maybe he'd be mad enough to throw himself down.

'It seems Noah had the same idea as Ruskin. Now listen. This is what we are going to do.'

Noah searched the man he'd killed, helping himself to the gun belt and Peacemaker and a sharp-bladed knife concealed in a boot sheath. He also took the few dollars the man had stuffed into a back pocket. And the boots were his size!

Cautiously he looked down. They were spreading out. Setting up look-out spots around Needle's Point. They intended to starve him out.

There was water up here, trapped deep down within the jagged cracked rocks that made up the top of this place. If he reached down, putting his arm down as far as he could reach, he was able to scoop up a handful.

His gaze fell on the bloodied remains of the man he'd just beaten to death. His stomach heaved. The thought revolted him, disgusted him but it was a way to stave of starvation, away to stay alive a mite longer while he tried to figure out what the hell to do. Flies were beginning to swarm around him and the man he'd killed, drawn in by the smell of blood.

Stunted shrubs grew up here. Some were dead and tinder-dry. He tried to think. Maybe he needed to get some kind of a small fire going. Maybe he ought to have a try at drying out a few strips of meat. But he would need to cut them off the carcass. His stomach heaved again. His situation was enough to drive anyone mad. Hell, he ought to have stayed put. He ought never have headed to the frontier in search of a new life. He took hold of the knife. The blade was razor-sharp. With a muffled curse he took hold of the carcass. Sure as hell he did not know what he had done to deserve this!

Theodore Black decided not to waste his time waiting for Mr Noah to die. He left some of his men as look-outs and headed back to his ranch. 'Keep your mouth shut about this!' he once again warned his son.

Noah had managed to get a fire going. Laboriously he dried strips of meat over the flame. He wasn't giving up and dying without fighting to stay alive. He would have never thought himself capable of this, which showed he did not know himself as well as he had thought.

Jericho had at last ridden out to the Brannigan farm and made himself known to his sister.

She glared at him. 'Well I always knew I'd a brother somewhere. But I never expected it to be you. There's plenty of work needing doing around here. If you intend to stay you'll do your share.'

He nodded.

'And don't you be saying Tom is the father of Dotty's baby because that ain't so. He's vowed he ain't.'

Jericho turned away, hiding a smile.

'Well, are you staying?' she yelled.

He shrugged. 'I reckon so.' He glanced up

at the sky. 'Seems likely we're gonna have rain.'

'A downpour is overdue,' she agreed.

'I see the town is rebuilding the school-house.'

She nodded. 'Word is they are going to employ a lady teacher. Folk think it will be quieter that way.' She gave a shrug. 'They'll not get a teacher to equal Mr Noah. I wish him well wherever he is.'

Noah reached for a maggot. Plenty were crawling over the remains of the man he knew now had been called Ruskin. The man had carried a faded photo of himself in younger days and his name was scrawled on the photo. Putting the maggot between his lips he chewed slowly. Maggots and dried-out pieces of what once had been Ruskin were keeping him going. His constitution must be a strong one for what he had been obliged to exist on was enough to poison him a hundred times over.

Down below the two-legged hyenas left behind by Theodore Black still kept guard, although by now Noah had lost all track of time. He had underestimated Black, for the man's vindictiveness was beyond measure. The hell of it was Noah knew he'd done nothing wrong. He was an innocent man. And still Black wanted him dead.

Overhead the sky darkened. A deluge ought to see the two-legged hyenas on their way, or so he hoped. Surely they would have given up on him by now? Surely they would think him dead? They would not reason that in his desperation to survive he had been obliged to make a meal of Ruskin. Such an act to a normal mind was too hideous to contemplate.

Thunder rumbled and lightning forked across the sky. Martin Pike, the senior man amongst the waddies Black had set to watch out for Noah, made a decision.

'Hell, he's dead!' Pike declared gloomily. 'The water has come too late to save him. He'll have perished from thirst and starvation. It ain't possible the varmint has survived.' He fell silent beneath the onslaught of the rain for some moments. Then he said, 'I'm getting out of here. He's dead, I say. I ain't catching pneumonia on account of Mr Noah. The boss himself would not keep vigil in this downpour, I can tell you!' And with that Pike mounted his horse and headed for home. After a moments hesitation the other men followed his lead. Theodore Black could rant all he liked but this foolishness was over. Mr Noah had to be dead.

Noah closed his eyes, hoping fiercely that the deluge would drive them away. He'd endured unremitting heat for days on end, together with long cold nights. He stunk to high heaven. His hair had become filthy and matted. And now, soaked to the bone, he cursed Theodore Black and his son. One day soon those varmints were going to run out of luck. He gritted his teeth. If fate didn't deal with them he'd do it himself.

The downpour continued seemingly end-lessly, and then it ceased as abruptly as it had started. Steam rose from the ground. And the citizens of Hawk's Head, who had mostly been obliged to stay under cover, began to emerge.

'Hell, it sure was a downpour,' Clem Sawyer exclaimed. But he wasn't complain-ing. He was back in favour with Miz Polly who had been keeping him company at the jail while the rain fell. And now she was back yelling that he had to see to it that the doc attended Dotty Glover.

'Fetch him back at the point of a gun if needs be,' she ordered.

Grumbling, Sawyer set out to get the doc.

He noticed that the travelling gunman did not seem to be armed. He dismissed the man from his mind.

Across Main Street a middle-aged Mexican woman in man's attire was loading supplies on to a packhorse. Sawyer knew who she was although he had never known her name. She scratched out a living up in the hills, raising goats and then sold them to various restaurants in the towns within travelling distance. He dismissed her from his mind. She wasn't important. He forgot about the woman. What mattered now was getting the doc to Dotty Glover. He'd get the medic to the laundry even if he needed to put a Peacemaker to the man's head. He didn't care a damn about Dotty Glover but a riled Miz Polly was another matter.

Tom Brannigan, who was sweet on Dotty Glover, had managed to give his ma and his newly discovered uncle the slip. He stared longingly at the door of Miz Polly's laundry, trying to summon up courage to brave the old dragon and demand to see Dotty.

'You show your face here and I'll make you eat a bar of soap,' she had threatened last time she'd caught him hanging around the laundry.

Across Main Street someone yelled out an

insult concerning Dotty Glover. Tom knew who it was. There, lounging against a hitching post, was a grinning Freddy Black. Tom didn't hesitate. He sprinted across Main Street and punched Freddy Black on the mouth. Freddy staggered back and then waded in, fists flying.

Clem Sawyer coming back with the doc arrived just as townsmen were separating the two boys. The lawman gave a snort of disgust. 'Get him home to his pa,' he yelled, spotting one of Theodore's men. 'And you,' he pointed a finger at Tom Brannigan, 'you get home to your ma before I throw you in jail!' He propelled the doc into the laundry and promptly forgot about the two boys.

Angelina ignored a few disapproving looks directed her way and left town with her supplies. She was a goat-herder and had more sense than to wear skirts and voluminous petticoats. She saw the man when she reached the area where the towering pinnacle of rock known in town as Needle's Point was situated. There he was, stumbling along the tracks towards her. From beneath her poncho she drew her Peacemaker. But before she could challenge him he collapsed and lay face downwards in the dirt.

Common sense dictated that she left this stinking filthy bum to his fate but she hesitated. At heart she was a good woman. And if he showed any signs of being a threatening cuss she'd was capable of blasting him without hesitation.

CHAPTER 9

The voices were angry. They spoke rapidly in Spanish. He understood enough to know he was the subject of their conversation. He lay still, pretending to be unconscious, knowing his life could depend on what he could understand of the furious exchange. The first thing he worked out was that they were brother and sister and secondly, the man was berating his sister for bringing a stranger home and putting them at risk.

'You didn't worry about putting me at risk,' she replied angrily.

'You are a fool, sister,' the man snapped. 'This man cannot be trusted. He will talk. He will bring trouble to our door.'

Noah reckoned it was time to return to the land of the living. He opened his eyes. Two faces peered down at him.

'Drink!' The woman raised a cup to his lips. It was tepid soup. Chicken by the taste of it. Then he remembered just what he'd been obliged to do to stay alive, just what he'd been obliged to eat to save himself from starvation. His stomach rebelled against the soup!

'A few sips,' she encouraged. With an effort he managed to keep the soup down. His heaving stomach rebelled again and he pushed the soup away.

'My clothes?' he croaked.

'I've burnt those filthy stinking rags. My brother is the same size as you.'

As soon as he was able Noah aimed to get out of here. And then he remembered he'd be lost out in this wilderness. He was a city man, unable to navigate his way around this vast expanse of nothingness. He couldn't survive out here alone because he'd wander around hopelessly lost until thirst, starvation and exhaustion finished him off. He was dependent on these folk and he didn't like it one bit.

A second woman entered the room, tall and dignified with greying hair pinned back in a pleat. He clamped his jaws shut as he stifled his exclamation of surprise. The last time he'd seen this woman she'd been wearing a fancy bonnet and was being driven in style in a fancy carriage. What in tarnation was she doing here?

There was no recognition in her eyes. She didn't know him. They'd never spoken. Why would they? He was just riff-raff from the worst side of town. What the hell, he asked himself, was the wife of Judge Elmore Standish doing here, wherever here was?

She frowned slightly and then smiled as the grey-haired Mexican slipped an arm possessively around her waist.

'Goddamnit!' Noah croaked. He understood. She was Judge Elmore Standish's wife. And this galoot looked like Judge Elmore Standish's hired help. She'd run off with the hired help. There couldn't be any other reason for her presence here. His throat hurt like hell it was so sore, but he was able to speak. 'He'll find you. You know that. He won't give up. He'll pay an army of hirelings to search until he's tracked you down. And then he'll come after you.'

'He knows!' the man exclaimed. A knife appeared in his hand, light glinting on its blade.

'Put that away,' Noah ordered. He took a gulp of tepid water. 'I'm in danger now same as you. I've already crossed your husband once. I threw your son out of Flannigan's Bar. He was up to no good!' He took another gulp. 'If the judge finds me here he'll string me up alongside the rest of you.' He glared at the Mexican. 'That's if we are lucky! I've heard plenty concerning Elmore Standish. He's a mean-hearted varmint!'

'He can't find us here!' Mrs Elmore Standish declared, sounding as though she was trying to convince herself.

'Hell, maybe he has already,' Noah rejoined wearily. He sank back against the pillow.

'Brother, you should never have come home,' the Mexican woman rebuked. 'We are dead. All of us!'

'No.' Noah forced himself to sit upright. The room swam round him. 'Give me some more soup. We've got to make preparation, that's what we've got to do. We'll find a way. We'll find a way to deal with Elmore Standish.'

'What way?' the Mexican woman questioned.

'It's them or us.' He took another sip of soup. 'If there are ways we can find to stay alive we'll figure them out. I ain't survived Needle's Point to die here, put down by Judge Elmore Standish.' He waved the soup away. 'Now help me up. I need to have a look around. I need to figure something out.' From their faces he knew they hadn't figured out a damn thing between them. All they'd done was rely on the judge not being able to track Mrs Standish down.

'Just look at that!' Miz Polly declared. She was on the sidewalk with Clem Sawyer. They both stared at the approaching cavalcade. The men and their horses had disembarked from the train. The group were clearly Easterners. Polly was mighty glad she was wearing a respectable bonnet, the brim of which concealed her face, because she recognized two members of the cavalcade. One of them was Judge Elmore Standish himself, and the handsome fair-haired young man riding beside the judge was his son. She'd never had any personal dealings with either of them although she knew who they were.

For one foolish moment she thought they were after Mr Noah. She remembered Noah saying that he'd been obliged to leave town to escape thugs sent by Judge Elmore Standish, the very man who had laid charges against her, accusing her of stealing Nathaniel's watch. She couldn't remember a damn thing about that fateful night other than Flannigan's bad-mouthing her and telling her to get out of town. Her heart thumped. She expected Nathaniel to point her out and denounce her as a thief. This was nonsense, she knew. The cavalcade swept by, the men glanced at her but she saw no sign of recognition on any face.

She looked different now. She was wearing a bonnet and a drab blue gingham dress with long sleeves and a high neck, sleeves she was obliged to roll up when working the laundry tubs but that was the way it had to be. She had to blend in. She had to look respectable. She didn't want anyone even thinking that she looked the kind of woman able to kill Edgar Smith. Thankfully folk around here seemed to have forgotten about Edgar's demise, but it was wise to take care.

Nathaniel Standish didn't recognize her. He'd long forgotten the drunken woman he'd been trying to abduct from Flannigan's Bar, although he had not forgotten the presumptuous bartender who had attacked him. The cowardly cur had got away. And then shortly after the fracas at the bar Nathaniel's mother had run away with the Mexican hired help. The judge had gone crazy. Nathaniel had feared for his father's sanity. But the judge had rallied; the murderous rage that had consumed him had sustained him during the time it had taken his hirelings to track the pair to this god-forsaken place. The Mexican was due to die a lingering death and arrangements had been put in hand to despatch Nathaniel's mother to an asylum.

They swept past the gawking fat lawman without stopping to explain their business. They halted outside the shabby-looking hotel, some cracking jokes about the standard of the place they were now obliged to patronize.

Clem shifted uncomfortably: if he were a better kind of lawman he would go along and demand to know what business this hunting party had with his town. But he was the kind of lawman who really didn't want to know when trouble was brewing.

'Now you keep away from those folk,' Miz Polly warned. 'They look to be nothing but trouble and there is enough trouble in the world without looking for it.' He nodded his agreement.

'He's dead I tell you!' Pike regarded his boss's son with annoyance. 'Or near enough as to make no difference,' he concluded wearily. The boss was in town, so he had found himself grilled by young Freddy Black.

'What do you mean "or near enough as makes no difference"?' Freddy demanded.

'He'll be nothing but bone. Out of his mind. Dying.' Pike shook his head, 'He's already dead, kid.'

'Well, he had better be. Now go and saddle me a horse will you, Pike?'

'Yes sir.' The sarcasm was lost on Freddy. He was heading out to see his friend Hughie. Hughie was none too bright. More important, Hughie's boots were falling to pieces and he would be glad to earn the money. If anyone was fool enough to climb Needle's Point, it was Hughie.

In the private room of the Cattlemen's Hotel Theodore Black lit a cigar. He wondered what had brought these Easterners to his town. For one crazy moment he thought Mr Noah was in some way connected to their arrival, but Mr Noah was a nobody, after all, and these men were clearly gentlemen.

Freddy Black scowled. He had been forced to pay more than he had wanted. And it was not Hughie climbing Needle's Point but Hughie's sister.

'I daren't,' Hughie had blubbed.

'I'll do it. Give me the money.' Hughie's sister had stared up at the rock face, tucked her skirts into her drawers and begun to climb. Wound over her shoulder was a long rope to help her get back down again.

Freddy held his breath, expecting Mr Noah to appear over the rim of the rock face, shooter in hand ready to blast the lot of them. Nothing happened and on reaching the top she disappeared from sight.

The girl looked around. Spotting a sturdy-looking tree that had sprouted up she tied one end of the rope around the trunk. She took care to make sure the knot was secure.

'You see anything?' Freddy yelled when, after what seemed hours, she was back on firm ground.

'Well, Mr Noah ain't up there. It can't be him. He can't have chopped off his own head. Take a look!' She tipped something out of the sack she'd brought down with her, and had the satisfaction of seeing Freddy turn green.

Putrid bits of flesh still adhered to the skull, this thing that had once been somebody's head.

Mouth gaping, Freddy stared. These remains couldn't belong to Mr Noah. He suddenly remembered old Ruskin. Mr Noah must have cut off Ruskin's head. But where was the rest of Ruskin and where was

Mr Noah?

'Come on, Hughie,' the girl nudged her elder brother. 'We're headed home. If Pa finds out I've climbed Needle's Point there will be hell to pay. We ain't supposed to wander alone.'

Freddy grabbed up the skull and stuffed it into the sack. He was afraid to be left alone. He half-expected Mr Noah to jump out of the scrub. He knew the schoolteacher was capable of throttling the life out of him.

'Are you sure?' he yelled.

The girl looked at him. 'Yes. There are bones up there with no meat left on them. And there's water. Who did he eat, Freddy?'

Freddy ignored the question. He got on his horse and rode after the other two. He wasn't going to look for Mr Noah alone. He needed his pa. He had to tell his pa that Mr Noah wasn't dead like Pike had said.

'Elmore Standish will hunt you down,' Noah reiterated once again. 'He has to keep his position of respect. This man will not let others turn him into a laughing-stock. I know the man has not got any honour to start with, but you have dishonoured him in the eyes of his peers. He'll want to get even. I've heard plenty about that man and none of it's been good.'

'So you say,' the Mexican woman, Angelina, repeated. Manuel, her brother, nodded. 'But you are asking us to make our home uninhabitable. You are asking us to live amongst the rocks, forego shelter and comfort. And you cannot say for how long. Our sacrifices will all be for nothing if you are wrong about him finding us.'

'We all four of us want to keep on breathing,' Noah rejoined. 'I am determined on this. I aim to catch that varmint and his hunting party by surprise.'

'His hunting party!' Angelina exclaimed.

'His gentlemen friends,' Noah replied patiently. 'They'll see it as an adventure. Now, rattlers,' he continued, 'rattlers is what we need!'

Angelina sighed. 'Your ordeal has driven you mad, Mr Noah. Nevertheless I will help you find your rattlers.'

Nathaniel Standish found the hotel boring. 'I think I'll visit the saloon.'

'Sit down,' his father ordered. 'You can visit the saloon when our business is concluded.'

Nathaniel smiled. He sat down. He could visit the saloon when the old man turned in for the night.

'Don't even think about it, Nathaniel. We don't need trouble. Not right now,' his father said, emphasizing the words. He stared at his son. His voice was low. 'You know what I mean!'

Uncertainly Nathaniel sat down. Suddenly he was not so sure of himself. He began to wonder just how much the old man knew about certain matters, murdered women of no account, women who wouldn't be missed, women who, if they turned up dead in an alleyway, were deemed to be responsible themselves for whatever had happened to them.

He smiled unpleasantly. The red-headed woman whose face he could not even remember had indeed had a lucky escape. And so had the damn bartender!

Judge Standish sipped his brandy. He caught the eye of another occupant of the private room. The man nodded. The judge did not trouble himself to respond although the man stretched out in a comfortable chair, cigar in hand, was probably an important somebody around here.

Theodore Black was prevented from dwelling on the snub by a loud commotion outside the door. He recognized his son's voice high and agitated. What now, he thought wearily; with Freddy it was always one thing after another.

Freddy Black tussled with the desk clerk. 'We've important folk enjoying our facilities,' the man hissed. 'Take a look in the mirror. Get yourself cleaned up. Your pa won't be pleased to see you in such a state.'

'You button your lip,' Freddy yelled. 'You don't know what my pa wants. You no-account bum. My pa owns this town.' Freddy kicked the clerk, causing the man to loosen his grip. Having twisted free Freddy rushed to deliver the news of his discovery to his pa.

He burst into the private backroom of the Cattlemen's Hotel. He didn't care that his clothes were torn and that filth and dirt smeared his face and hands. He scarcely noticed the sea of eyes fixed on him, some of those eyes openly scornful and disgusted, others simply amused. He scarcely noticed his father's fury as he blurted out his news with no regard to who heard.

'It's Mr Noah. He ain't done for. He's still alive!'

'What's he yapping about!' an elderly rancher exclaimed. 'I saw him get on that goddamn train myself. Damn pity he couldn't stay around until the schoolhouse got rebuilt. Yep, he was a might fine teacher.'

'It's Pike's doing. He ran for home first sign of rain,' Freddy gabbled. 'But I checked it out. Noah went mad. He's eaten Ruskin!'

'What are you saying, boy?' the rancher exclaimed.

'He did, Pa. He even took off Ruskin's head. See!' Freddy opened the sack. 'Look, Pa!'

'Goddamnit,' Theodore roared, recovering his wits. He snatched the sack from Freddy. 'We'll talk outside, boy.' He propelled his fool of a son towards the door. His voice shook with fury. His damn fool of a son might as well have announced to the whole town what had been going on. He could not quite believe that Freddy possessed the guts to climb Needle's Point. 'Mr Noah!' The judge raised an eyebrow. He recalled the Mr Noah who had humiliated his son before speedily leaving the city.

'Mr Noah, our schoolteacher,' an old rancher replied. He rubbed his jaw. 'A mighty fine man. Mr Noah decided to leave on account of the schoolhouse burning down. I saw him get on the train myself.' He headed for the door. 'Let's see what Sawyer has to say about this,' he muttered.

'Have you no sense, boy?' Theodore shook

his son violently. His fingers dug into Freddy's shoulders. 'Don't you know when to keep your mouth shut? Do you want me branded as the man who killed Mr Noah?'

'But he ain't dead, Pa. That's what I'm trying to tell you,' Freddy gabbled.

'You're a fool, boy, and you can't be trusted. Now lower your voice and tell me what this is about. You can start by telling me who climbed Needle's Point and brought the head back on down.'

This was not the reception Freddy had been expecting, He'd been expecting thanks.

'Discretion boy, discretion,' Theodore muttered. 'When will you learn sense?'

'That damn bartender turned up here in Hawk's Head!' Nathaniel exclaimed.

'It seems so.' The judge nodded. 'If you will excuse me, gentlemen, I must have a few words with the father and son.' He smiled sardonically. 'The boy is clearly a disappointment and a liability and a burden to his father. I can almost feel sorry for the man!'

He left the hotel. The two he was looking for were still outside, the rancher glowering and the son sullen.

'I believe we may have a mutual problem,' the judge declared. 'Although to me the man has merely proved an irritant. Get home, young man. You need to bathe and change your clothes, while I need to speak to your father.' The judge paused. 'You will, of course, bury whatever is in that sack.'

'Get home, Freddy, and do as he says,' Theodore yelled.

'But Pa, I want to come along.'

'No. Wait at the ranch, I say.' Theodore kept his voice raised. 'Go, before I do something we will both regret.' He slowly clenched and unclenched his fists, thinking that word of what had happened inside the hotel would spread throughout the town.

All was not lost. Clem Sawyer was such a lazy no-account bum that he would not trouble himself looking into matters occuring outside his jurisdiction. No one had seen the head except himself. The matter could be tidied up by ensuring Mr Noah was well and truly dead and that his body was never found.

'I'm Judge Elmore Standish.' The other man introduced himself.

'Theodore Black,' the rancher replied, wondering why the high and mighty judge had decided to acknowledge him after all. It had to be, he realized, connected with the varmint Mr Noah.

CHAPTER 10

Freddy Black was peeved that his pa had left town with Judge Elmore Standish. He was more than peeved that he hadn't been included in the hunt for Mr Noah. But his pa's absence did have a certain advantage. Freddy had come up with a plan to settle the score with Tom Brannigan. Smithers, the ramrod, would be easy enough to fool.

Right now Smithers was on his way to carry out instructions regarding Pike, the no-good who had let Mr Noah slip away.

Freddy tagged along as Smithers headed for the bunkhouse. The incensed ramrod hauled Pike from his bunk and then promptly smashed the man in the face whilst he berated him for not making sure Mr Noah was done for.

'Now the boss has been forced to go and put right your mess,' Smithers bawled as he booted Pike for good measure.

Pike had more sense than to try and fight back. He lay sobbing on the floor.

'On your belly, crawl out of here like the

no-account bum you are,' Smithers yelled. 'You're fired. And the rest of you, when the boss gives an order you follow it to the letter. That way you and me will get along real fine.'

Freddy delighted in witnessing Pike's painful humiliation. He watched as Pike, clutching his saddle horn, hauled himself on to his horse and, lurching from side to side, rode away.

'We've got a ranch to keep going whilst the boss is away,' Smithers declared. And that was what he was going to do. He damn well knew better than to accept any orders issued by that young fool Freddy.

That Mr Noah had eaten Ruskin said much for Noah's ruthless determination to stay alive. Smithers tried to squash the vague unease he felt whenever he thought about Mr Noah. The devil looked after his own, they said, and the devil so far had looked after Mr Noah!

Noah dipped a piece of hard bread into the gravy. His stomach still churned at the sight of meat. His throat clenched every time he tried to swallow. He doubted whether he'd ever want to eat meat again. He found it hard to put thoughts of Ruskin from his mind.

Mrs Standish had confided that fear had driven her to bolt with Manuel. They'd been caught together by one of the servants whom she had paid to keep quiet. But she'd known it was only a matter of time before the judge learned what had been going on.

And so they had come here to Manuel's sister, to this wilderness. And she persisted in believing they would be safe.

'Really, Mr Noah,' she grumbled, 'how long must we huddle in this disgusting tent. It's most unseemly. Women need their privacy!'

'Do you want to be skinned alive, Manuel?' Noah yelled at Manuel who was nodding his agreement. 'What about your sister! You've brought death to her door. And you, Mrs Standish, why I guess he'll pack you off to a lunatic asylum for the rest of your days. That's a good way of explaining away your crazy behaviour.' He shook his head. 'There's nothing for it. We've got to dispose of the whole darn bunch of them, that's what we've got to do. They'll be coming. He won't leave this be. It's them or us. Now which one of you women is going to be the first to keep watch? I can trust you to do that, can't I?'

'I will keep watch,' Angelina replied. 'If you are right, Mr Noah, you will have saved us.' She cast a glance at her brother. 'Time

154

will tell!'

Smithers sat in the boss's office. His boots rested on the desk, a cigar was clamped between his teeth. It felt good to be in charge.

When Freddy burst into the room Smithers felt obliged to remove his boots from the desk. 'Well, what is it?' he asked.

'My friend Hughie,' Freddy gasped, clearly out of breath. 'He say's he saw Tom Brannigan butchering one of our steers.'

'The hell you say.' Smithers came to his feet. 'You're sure of this!'

'On my pa's life,' Freddy replied without hesitation. 'What are we going to do?' he asked slyly, knowing better than to press Smithers to take action.

'Hell, I know what we are going to do,' Smithers yelled. 'We're going to do just what your pa would do.' He shook his head. 'Seems what happened to Dobbs has not learned those no-accounts. They're still taking liberties!'

Freddy nodded his agreement. 'Can I come along to represent my pa?'

'Sure. But keep your lips buttoned and leave it all to me,' the ramrod rejoined.

'Yes sir,' Freddy replied smartly. Smithers regarded him suspiciously but the youngster didn't appear to be joshing. Maybe having seen how Pike had been dealt with had made an impression.

As Smithers strode out of the house, Freddy at his heels, he missed seeing the smirk that spread across Freddy's face.

Jericho was tired of hearing about the late Tom Brannigan, young Tom's pa. The late Mr Brannigan, he'd been told more times than he wanted to hear, had always suffered from a delicate constitution. He'd been a scholarly man whose ambition had been for young Tom to go East and study medicine. And then his brother-in-law had died, leaving young Tom and his ma to fend for themselves.

Jericho headed for the barn. His sister and nephew were starting to argue again about Dotty Glover.

'It's you, Ma!' Tom yelled. 'You told Miz Polly to keep me out of the laundry.'

Jericho clambered up in the hayloft. His brother-in-law had also liked to escape to the barn. He'd liked to make things. Jericho conceded that the man had been good at making things. And this contraption that he'd made would have taken a hell of a lot of time. The more he studied it the more he saw that it had been positioned just right.

His sister swept into the barn and began to get the buggy ready. 'I'm going into town. I guess it's time I spoke to Dotty. Miz Polly says Dotty has not been driven mad by her ordeal so perhaps it's time her and me had a word!'

'I'll keep an eye on things.'

'Mind that you do.'

Jericho went into the house. 'Get out there and clean the pigs out, Tom. Since I've been here you've been idling around thinking about that girl. Hell, I bet Dotty Glover ain't thinking about you.'

Tom almost yelled out that Jericho should shut his mouth but the look on his uncle's face caused him to remember that his uncle was a hired killer, after all. Wisely he decided to clean the pigs out.

His uncle went back into the barn. Half-heartedly Tom got on with the task. All he could think about these days was Dotty and the baby recently delivered by the doc. Word was that Clem Sawyer had threatened to shoot the doc unless he attended Dotty.

Tom was leaning on his pitchfork when he first noticed the approaching riders. As they drew nearer, he recognized the big galoot as Theodore Black's ramrod. And Freddy was with them as well. Tom began to feel uneasy and he wished his pa were here. He glanced towards the barn expecting Jericho to appear but there was no sign of his uncle.

'Maybe he ain't such a big man.' Tom muttered. Maybe Uncle Jericho was running scared. Tom was scared himself now but then he wasn't a top gun supposedly immune to fear.

He could run for the house and try to get the old shotgun but he knew they could shoot him down whilst he was running. And his legs, much to his shame, were shaking. He remembered what had happened to Dobbs. But he had nothing to fear. He had done nothing wrong. He hadn't helped himself to their steers.

Jericho frowned. The men riding in were not coming to exchange pleasantries. A man named Dobbs had been hanged recently hereabouts, he recalled.

He wondered whether his nephew had been wide-looping, helping himself to an occasional steer. It was a risky business and not something a youngster would engage in normally. Jericho didn't give a damn whether his nephew had stolen beef. But these men were here for something!

Idly he studied the object in the barn.

Surprise was always an advantage. This business had to be concluded pretty damn quick, before his nephew was hurt.

'Ma ain't here,' Tom exclaimed foolishly. Two of the riders had peeled away and were heading for the smoke house, a kind of lean-to where they smoked their meat.

'It ain't your ma we want to see, boy!' the hard-eyed ramrod told him. 'We've been told you've been helping yourself to Mr Black's beef.'

'That's a lie. Who told you? He's lying. Freddy is lying.'

'It ain't Freddy accusing you, boy.' He gestured to one of the waddies. 'If there ain't no evidence you'll have my apology but–'

'Got it, boss,' the waddy yelled, from the smoke house. 'Damn fool ain't even got rid of the hide.'

'I never put it there. It was him.' Tom pointed at Freddy. 'He did it.' His voice shook. They didn't believe him.

'Freddy didn't frame you, boy,' Smithers replied.

'I'm innocent.'

'Your age won't save you,' the ramrod continued. 'Mr Black does not make exceptions. If you are old enough to butcher a steer you are old enough to hang. Get out the hanging rope!'

Tom stood as though turned to stone; he'd forgotten about Jericho, his only thought was that they were going to hang him, probably from that old tree growing alongside the house.

Jericho finished his preparations.

Tom sank to his knees. He was so damn scared he couldn't even pray. Like a mesmerized rabbit he stared at the hanging rope.

Freddy had never thought it would be so easy. He'd put Hughie up to it. He'd paid Hughie to plant the hide and meat in Mrs Brannigan's smoke house. Hughie hadn't even butchered the steer. Freddy had got the meat and hide from his own smoke house. Hughie wouldn't be fool enough to blab. Hughie wouldn't incriminate himself.

Jericho pulled the lever. The hod of the catapult flew forward with considerable force, sending its collection of missiles raining down on the hanging party. Ammunition was plentiful. There were buckets filled with nuts and bolts, twisted pieces of rail, jagged stones and plenty of broken bottles.

The onslaught had the desired effect, with horses going crazy and sending men tumbling to the ground. Jericho came out of the barn with guns blazing. When he'd seen the meat and hide being brought from the smoke house he'd known there was no peaceful way out of this mess. Words couldn't save Tom. Only slugs could help his nephew.

His first slug took out the big boss, blowing off the top of the man's head. Automatically the gunman shot to kill, planting his slugs where they would do most harm. 'Freeze,' he bellowed. 'Freeze!' Four men, including the ramrod, were dead. The others didn't even try to take on Jericho.

Tom wanted to vomit. He'd never seen so much blood. One of the dead men had knelt for a moment, holding the gaping wound in his stomach before keeling over to lie face down on the bloodstained dirt.

'I never stole their steer,' Tom babbled, finding his voice.

'I don't give a damn if you did,' Jericho said. 'No one strings up my kin. Not while I am breathing.'

'But it was there. In the smoke house,' Tom babbled. 'And I never put it there.'

'So who did?' Jericho eyed young Freddy Black. 'Was it you? Because if it was men are dead on account of you.'

'It was Hughie. He told on you,' Freddy

yelled frantically. 'I only did what was right. I only told Smithers what Hughie told me. I'm not to blame.'

Jericho eyed the men still living. He was going to take a gamble on this. 'Well, I'm going to do what's right. You men take Freddy over to see this Hughie. Maybe Hughie's pa will encourage Hughie to tell the truth regarding this matter. Maybe you'll need a word or two with young Freddy here regarding your dead pards. As for me, I'm taking these bodies into town. I need to square things with Clem Sawyer.'

'I'm Freddy Black,' Freddy yelled. 'You hurt me and you'll have my pa to deal with.'

'Get out of here, you varmints,' the gunman ordered and they went. None of them had any fight left in them. He watched as they rode away and then turned towards his nephew.

'I'm innocent,' Tom yelled. 'I never touched Theodore Black's steer and ... and I never touched Dotty Glover.'

'You were going to let them hang you without even lifting a finger to try and save yourself,' Jericho accused. 'You were frozen with fear, kneeling, snivelling. I'm staying around. I've got to put you on the right path. If you go down, Tom, you go down fighting aiming to take others with you. Your ma has done her best. I'll concede she's done her best, but you ain't learned what you need to know. Furthermore you won't be any damn use to Dotty Glover or any other female until you are able to defend yourself and your kin. Understood?'

Tom nodded.

'Quit snivelling. We're headed to town. We need to clear these killings with Clem Sawyer.'

'We'll return to the ranch,' Freddy ordered. 'My pa will be home soon. He'll deal with that killer.'

'I know him,' one of the waddies observed quietly. 'He is called Jericho and he is poison. You set us on Jericho's kin. Good men have died today. Tie him up.'

Two of the waddies were happy to oblige, securing Freddy before he realized their intention.

'I'm Theodore Black's son,' he yelled desperately, 'You hurt me and my pa will hunt you down. You'll see.'

'As to what happens to you, Freddy, that all depends on what Hughie has to say. His pa don't countenance liars. He'll get the truth out of Hughie.'

'You harm me and you'll pay,' Freddy yelled.

'You're talking as though you know Hughie is gonna admit the whole thing was a damn lie thought up by you. You sure as hell fooled Smithers, you little varmint.' The waddy paused. 'As for harming you, ain't none of us going to harm a hair on your head. I'll vouch for that.'

Freddy felt better. They would tell his pa, that was all. Pa would bawl him out maybe even lash out but he knew his pa would never really hurt him.

'The man's a bartender,' Judge Standish had informed Theodore Black. 'He mixed with the dregs of society. How he fooled this town into thinking he was the schoolteacher you had hired I do not know. They share the same name, that is for sure, but the real Mr Noah was clearly a gentleman. Noah Swan is no better than garbage from the gutter. He's a no-good. And he made fools out of you all. If you want Mr Noah ride along with us, Mr Black. My tracker will find him for you.'

Instinct told Theodore not to enquire as to exactly why Judge Elmore Standish had travelled West with his hunting party. He hadn't come to Hawk's Head searching for

164

Mr Noah. He hadn't even known Noah had hit town. He had nodded. 'I'll accept your invite. I'm looking for a quick solution. I'm a ranching man, after all.'

The judge had nodded. 'The matter should not take long to resolve,' he had said, adding significantly, 'You're not a squeamish man, are you, Mr Black? There's no place for a squeamish man in my party.'

They were at Needle's Point now and the tracker was circling round whilst the gentlemen hunters smoked their cigars. Theodore curbed his impatience; his inclination was to boot the tracker and tell the man to get moving but the judge seemed content to wait. And Elmore Standish was running this show. A fact Theodore knew he would be foolish to forget.

Dotty Glover lay in a small room at the back of the laundry. Next to her, wrapped in white sheeting, her baby boy slept.

Miz Polly had never asked Dotty what she wanted. 'You can have a job at the laundry,' Miz Polly had offered. 'That way you can earn enough to support yourself and the baby and to hell with the sanctimonious grizzlers in this town.'

Dotty had kept quiet. There was no point

in telling Miz Polly this wasn't the life she wanted. She could hear Miz Polly and an excited customer.

'Hell, Miz Polly,' the man yelled loudly, 'that no-account bum Jericho has ridden into town with four dead bodies. It seems Theodore Black's men tried to hang young Tom on a trumped-up charge of rustling. Theodore himself is off hunting Mr Noah.'

'What the hell are you saying?' Miz Polly exclaimed.

'Noah was thrown off the train, Miz Polly. Ain't word reached you yet? Sure as hell Clem Sawyer knows something has been going on. Young Freddy caused a ruckus at the hotel.'

Miz Polly yelling out that Dotty was to mind the laundry, headed for Sawyer's office.

Dotty peeped out of the laundry door. The whole town seemed to be headed for Clem Sawyer's office.

There was another train leaving today. Any time now! She stuffed a change of clothing into a valise, found a bonnet and cloak, helped herself to the cash Miz Polly had thoughtfully left stuffed under a mattress. Then Dotty slipped out of the back door and headed for the station.

She left the baby behind.

The ticket clerk sold her a one-way ticket without comment. Heart thudding, she boarded the train. She sank back against the upholstery, exhausted by the effort of getting away.

Theodore Black and the hunting party were some distance from the railway track. They heard the faint sound of the whistle as the train rounded Needle's Point. There'd been no sign of Mr Noah. Faint tracks had been found heading upwards towards the hills.

'Seems he is headed into the hills,' the judge had observed dismissively, as if Noah were of little consequence. 'We're headed that way ourselves, so there's a good chance of running down Mr Noah. What do you say, rancher Black? Are you tagging along?'

Theodore Black had never tagged along in his life. He considered himself a leader of men. He nodded, trying to conceal his anger from the judge.

Also he was concerned about Freddy. Hell, it was time the boy put his nose to the grindstone and began to learn just what it took to run a ranch of considerable size and prosperity. He hoped he could trust Smithers to keep Freddy in line.

CHAPTER 11

Freddy had been found out. Hughie had blabbed. He'd been too scared to lie to his father. The whole story had come spilling out, how they had taken the hide and beef from Freddy's own smoke house and concealed it in Tom Brannigan's smoke house. Hughie had grizzled that he hadn't wanted to do it but Freddy had threatened him.

'Get out of my sight,' Hughie's enraged pa had yelled. 'I can't trust myself to be around you at the moment.' Snuffling, Hughie had bolted. Freddy wished he could do the same. But his father's men had kept him tied up.

'You little varmint,' one of the men said accusingly. 'We rode out to hang Jericho's kin on your say-so. Smithers was a good man. We saw Jericho's slug take off the top of his head. He believed you, Freddy. We believed you were telling the truth. You sent us out to hang an innocent man. What have you got to say?'

'You men can have the wages owing to the men killed by Jericho,' Freddy gabbled. 'My

168

pa will make it up to you.' They were nodding. Freddy, cheered, continued, 'No one in town knew the Brannigans were kin to Jericho. I couldn't know. Tom Brannigan never said.'

'You don't give a damn about Smithers and the other three men killed. You mangy little cur.' A gag was stuffed into his mouth. He struggled wildly as they pulled off one of his boots.

'You can't be shot or strung up as you deserve,' one of the men observed. 'Your pa might start asking awkward questions. Now if you were to be bit by a scorpion that's another matter, and it's a fitting way for a poisonous little varmint such as yourself to take his leave.'

At first Freddy didn't understand. He couldn't believe they intended to kill him.

'Look around for a scorpion,' the one who had taken charge ordered. Nonchalantly he rolled himself a smoke. 'The men who work for your pa ain't paid highly, just enough to have a good time once a month, maybe send money home to kin, and then it's a return to back-breaking work, out in all weathers working our guts out while you, Freddy, take things easy.' He shook his head disgust. 'We ain't as stupid as you thought, Freddy,

See! We've found a scorpion.'

Freddy tried to yell out as the squirming scorpion was tipped into his boot. Silently he screamed, first in terror and then in pain as his bare foot was forced down into his fancy red boot. He felt the fierce sting of the scorpion.

'His foot will swell so much that whoever finds him will have to cut his boot off,' a man observed callously. They rolled smokes as they watched young Freddy die. Then they untied him, removed the gag and rode away.

'Me, I'm quitting the territory. I ain't staying around to face Theodore Black when he gets back home,' said one.

'Hell, he may not get back. Mr Noah is pretty lethal. That man would be a match for Jericho, I say. If it ever came to that,' averred another.

'Pity it ain't Theodore himself lying there. He ought to have left that schoolteacher be!' observed a third. There were murmurs of assent.

Angelina was hot, bored and thirsty. Her thoughts turned to Mr Noah. He was a handsome man, she thought. That Mr Noah didn't want to be here was obvious. And yet Mr Noah had made no attempt to steal a horse and leave.

She snapped her fingers. Because he couldn't! Mr Noah was an Easterner. He couldn't find his way around out here. Angelina decided she must indicate to Mr Noah that as he wouldn't be getting out of here for some time there was no reason why the two of them should not become better acquainted. And after a while maybe Mr Noah wouldn't want to head back East.

From her high vantage point overlooking the land stretched out far below she had a good all-round view. If anything stirred down there she would see it. She fumed, she was loath to idle away her day when there was work to be done. But...

Movement below caught her attention. Antlike specks were moving over the terrain, men on horses coming their way. She was on her feet in an instant, running towards her horse, desperate to get back to the others and raise the alarm. Noah was right. Judge Elmore Standish had found them.

Money, Judge Elmore Standish mused, was everything! Without money he would not have been able to track down his runaway wife. And it had helped that Manuel was a fool. In earlier days Manuel had mentioned his sister as the servants had sat in the judge's kitchen, taking their meals. He'd even mentioned the area where the sister and her stinking goats hung out. Bribery had elicited the information. He'd sent men out to find where the sister roosted. He could have sent killers to do the job but he'd rounded up certain of his gentlemen friends and organized a hunting party.

'I intend to teach the bartender a lesson before I kill him.' Nathaniel smirked. 'Assuming he's with the Mexicans.'

'Where else could he be? The tracker would have found his body by now,' his father replied.

'You'll have to get in line!' Theodore Black thought it time to exert his authority.

'Let's say we toss a coin?' Nathaniel suggested.

'Let's say we find him first!' Theodore snapped.

'I can't believe how he fooled you folk in Hawk's Head!' Nathaniel jibed.

Theodore shrugged. 'Mr Noah is full of surprises, but I guess you know that!'

'He'll be dead meat pretty soon.' Nathaniel scowled. 'What have you got planned for Manuel, Pa?'

The judge didn't bother to reply to his

son's question. His eyes were fixed on the thin ribbon of grey smoke that wound its way skyward. 'Remember I want them alive,' he stated harshly.

'What about the fun you promised us, Judge?' a companion asked.

'I'll let Manuel's sister run for her life. He can watch as we use her for target practice,' Standish rejoined with an unpleasant smile. 'And as for Manuel, by the time I have finished with him he'll be begging us to use him for target practice.' He did not mention his wife. Nor did any of the others. 'Now, gentlemen, keep a look-out. I believe we have the element of surprise, but never take anything for granted, I say.'

There were murmurs of agreement. Then, as they drew near to their quarry, the group fell silent. Eyes scanned their surroundings for signs of danger. Muscles tensed as they anticipated coming under attack. Nothing happened.

The rocky ground forced them to proceed slowly, increasing their danger. The shack itself was set back against the rock face. Water trickled down the rock and pooled in a natural basin. Goat droppings littered the ground. Judge Standish could not believe his wife had left their mansion for this dung heap. He clenched his teeth. She would pay.

The party dismounted and moved silently forward. They would rush the house, surprise and overwhelm whoever was inside. Theodore Black, remembering how Mr Noah had blasted the Glovers, deliberately positioned himself at the rear of the party. The truth was they hardly noticed. He wasn't the leader here. As far as they were concerned he was just a man who tagged along.

He didn't trust Mr Noah. If Mr Noah were indeed here with these people, Theodore had a hunch things wouldn't go as smoothly as the high and mighty Judge Standish seemed to think. Underestimating the one-time bartender could be fatal!

Nathaniel Standish noticed the big rancher wasn't in the lead, as might have been expected. The man was hanging back. Instinct made Nathaniel follow suit. But his father, in his eagerness to get vengeful hands upon his wife and the man she had run off with, surged ahead. Rage reddened his features as his hand pushed against the shack door. It swung open and the judge, with two companions, burst into the shack, weapons at the ready.

Theodore could not see what happened but curses and yells and screams alerted him to the fact that things had gone very wrong.

'My God,' a man exclaimed. Theodore knew him to be a respected banker. The man joined the manhunt simply to put adventure into a boring existence.

Theodore, shoving stunned gentlemen hunters out of the way, pushed his way through and entered the shack. He stared in disbelief. Hell, he knew Mr Noah was responsible for this. What he saw confirmed what he already knew. Mr Noah had one hell of a twisted mind. The man had set a trap to catch whoever burst into the place. Floorboards had been removed, and a deep hole had been dug. The hole had then been covered over by straw matting. The drop wasn't deep enough to kill anyone, maybe just deep enough to knock the breath out of them, but the rattlers ready and waiting in that hole were striking at the targets.

'For God's sake let's shoot those goddamn snakes,' Theodore yelled. No one else moved so he did the job himself.

'This isn't how it was meant to be,' a man muttered before burying his face in his hands.

Nathaniel Standish stood as though turned to stone. He made no move to help his pa.

'Let's get them out.' Theodore eyed the

moaning semiconscious men dispassionately.

'What shall we do?' someone asked.

'Let's get them out.' Theodore jumped down into the pit. There wasn't a rattle. He'd bagged the lot. 'Come on! Help me with the judge!'

'We'll get them, Father. We'll get them. I swear it,' Nathaniel yelled. He'd realized fighting words were called for.

'We can't leave them to die alone,' his father's oldest friend muttered as he knelt beside the stricken judge, his shoulders shaking as he tried to rein in his emotions.

Nathaniel knelt beside his father. He could not quite believe it had come this. His father was dying. And all he could think of was that all the wealth was going to be his. His father's closest friend, Walter Thompson, was praying.

'They're getting away!' the tracker observed. He had been looking around and had found fresh tracks.

Nathaniel sprang to his feet. He seized the man by his shirt, pulling him towards him. 'To hell with them. My father is dying.' With a violent shove he sent the man flying into the dirt. He then resumed his vigil beside his father.

'Make yourself useful, man,' a gentleman

ordered. 'We need food. The horses need attending to. Earn your fee.'

'Fee be damned,' another observed. 'The fool has led us into a trap.'

Silently the tracker kindled a fire. He set coffee to brew and put a stew on to simmer. It was going to be a long night.

'We must take it in turn to keep watch!' Theodore declared. 'Noah might take it into his head to attack the camp.' There were murmurs of agreement and some of the hunting party now looked far from enthusiastic. Theodore hid his contempt. These men had no stomach for the chase. They had not expected that certain among them would become casualties. They would have slaughtered the Mexican and his sister, and dispatched Mrs Standish to an asylum had it not been for Noah.

Fate and Judge Elmore Standish had made Mr Noah flee West. That Mr Noah had ended in Hawk's Head was damn bad luck.

Nathaniel stayed beside his father. He blamed Theodore Black. It had been Black who'd arranged to have Mr Noah drugged and dumped from an eastward-bound train.

Walter Thompson continued to pray, although thoughts of Mr Noah kept intruding. The man was devious and dangerous, far more dangerous than Judge Elmore Standish had comprehended. It occurred to Walter Thompson that they could not predict what other tricks this Mr Noah might have ready and waiting for them.

As the grey of dawn drove away the blackness of night Nathaniel knew his father was dead. The others stirred; cold and stiff, they were unaccustomed to the hardship of sleeping beneath the sky. The guide was already rekindling the fire and setting coffee to brew.

Theodore Black stood up and stretched.

'Hello the camp. Hello the camp,' a voice yelled. 'It's me, boss. It's Wright!'

'What the hell!' His heart sank. His man Wright would only be here if something was very wrong. He'd have Smithers' hide if anything had happened to Freddy. He'd been a fool to ride with the high and mighty judge. That no-good bum Mr Noah was not worth the time that had been spent trying to run him down. Hell, the man would keep running. He would not show his face in Hawk's Head again.

His breath seemed to leave him and his legs threatened to give way beneath him as Wright blurted out the news concerning Freddy. 'Jericho never touched the boy!' Wright gabbled. 'He was found some distance from the Brannigan spread. It seems he bolted. It seems he pulled on his boot and there was a scorpion inside.' Wright paused. 'Folk still can't believe Freddy tried to set up Tom Brannigan.'

'Get out of my way,' Theodore Black roared. 'Saddle my horse, you no-account bum,' he bellowed at the tracker, knowing his shaking hands prevented him from attending to the task himself.

No one spoke. It was clear to all that the rancher was on the verge of madness.

'I ought not to have listened to that damn fool judge,' Theodore yelled as he mounted his horse. 'I was a fool to trust that no-account bum, Smithers.'

'He couldn't have known that the Brannigan boy's uncle is a hired gun.' Wright felt compelled to defend Smithers whom he had liked. He just managed to jump aside as Theodore spurred his horse forward. As it was he went sprawling awkwardly in the dirt.

'I'm taking the judge and the others home,' Walter Thompson announced wearily. The fight and the urge to seek adventure had drained out of him during the vigil he'd endured as his friends died.

'I'll be accompanying you,' Nathaniel told him. 'It's the right thing to do. I've got to see the judge safely home. Vengeance must wait.'

'Seems like your hunt's concluded,' Wright observed.

'Not all of us are quitters!' Cameron Hull, big game hunter, spoke up. 'I've brought down charging lions, crazed hippos. Gentleman, I believe I can deal with a barman and a Mexican house-servant.' He looked around at them all. 'We will smell our quarry before we can see them, for I believe they have taken their goats with them.'

'I want paying now.' The tracker found his voice.

The game-hunter's eyes narrowed. 'Get out of here before I kill you. You're not worth a nickel. You let a good man walk into a trap.'

The tracker thought to argue. But then thought better of it. Silently he mounted his horse and rode away.

Cameron Hull waited until the man was a fair distance before slowly raising and sighting his fancy rifle. He stared along the barrel, carefully taking aim before he pulled the trigger. The sound of the gun resounded in the stillness of morning and the guide fell from his horse.

'I need the practice,' Hull drawled.

'Excellent shot,' Nathaniel Standish replied nonchalantly. 'You there!' He pointed at

Wright. 'Make yourself useful. Help me get my father and his friends decently covered. We must return to Hawk's Head with all possible speed.'

'Yes, sir.' Wright gulped, relieved that he was not going to be murdered himself.

From afar Noah heard the sound of the gunshot. He did not trouble himself wondering what they were firing at. He guessed some of them would turn back now. He hoped the judge and son had gone into the rattlesnake pit. But even without the influence of the murderous pair there would be those foolhardy enough to press on with the chase.

Soloman reckoned his boss, Mrs Dora Wallace, was mad. As her employee he was often forced to sit and listen while she ranted about one thing or another. The son of a former slave, Soloman did not consider himself to be part of this town. He kept his job by agreeing with every word Mrs Wallace uttered. 'Yes, ma'am,' he would mutter respectfully as he sat with head bowed, waiting for the outburst of the day to conclude.

According to the *Hawk's Head Gazette*, their town paper, nothing very much happened in their sleepy, happy little town. As the editor, she was a damn liar. According to Mrs Wallace most of the town had turned out to pay their respects at the funeral of Frederick Black.

With a sigh Soloman started the print run. He knew damn well there had been only a handful of people at the funeral. And that included Theodore Black, the Easterner Nathaniel Standish, and Mrs Dora Wallace, who'd attended to report on events.

He could have told this town plenty about Mrs Dora Wallace but he knew when to keep his mouth shut. It was true he only had hunches to go on. He reckoned Mrs Dora Wallace was a dangerous, vindictive woman.

'Looks like I've got to keep him.' Miz Polly was tired of folk asking her what was to become of Dotty's baby now the girl had left town without the infant. 'And damned hard work it is,' she would declare.

And as for Clem Sawyer, she wouldn't spit on him if he were on fire. He wouldn't lift a finger to try and help Mr Noah. He refused to leave town, his excuse being that he needed to be around should trouble hit town. He'd spoken with the Easterner and Theodore Black, who both declared they knew nothing about Mr Noah's whereabouts.

'Damnation!' she yelled. 'What the hell am I to do?' She didn't expect a reply as she was alone at the laundry.

'I believe I can tell you what you are going to do,' a deep voice said. Startled, she spun round. She was so damn tired she had not heard Theodore Black enter the laundry.

Across Main Street, Mrs Dora Wallace had spotted Theodore Black going into the laundry.

Her curiosity aroused, she slipped quietly into the laundry.

'What the hell do you want with this child?' she heard Miz Polly shout angrily.

'He's my son. I'm taking him.'

'The hell you are. I know about you. And your son Freddy.'

'Get out of my way before I knock you down,' Black thundered. 'You try for that derringer you've got concealed on your person, I'll blast your head off.'

Mrs Dora Wallace found herself hoping Miz Polly did indeed reach for the concealed derringer.

'But Dotty Glover let folk think Edward White the teacher was responsible,' Miz Polly rejoined. 'Are you saying Dotty was lying?'

'You damn fool. I spread that rumour. Dotty knew better than to contradict me.

183

She knew I'd wring her neck if she spoke out of turn.' He drew breath and lowered his tone. 'But things have changed. Freddy has gone. I have a new boy to raise now and I aim to raise him right.'

'You tarred and feathered Edward White.'

'No!'

'Then the Glovers did at your instigation.'

'No. Seth Glover wanted a shotgun wedding. But it was too late. Someone had already dealt with Edward White. But who gives a damn about a damned schoolteacher! Now get out of my way, you no-good whore. I know your kind. You're not raising my son.' Fists clenched he moved towards the stunned woman.

A shot rang out and Theodore Black fell forward. He landed face down on the floor. Blood stained the back of his shirt. The little Glover baby began to bawl again as Polly gawked at her unlikely saviour.

'I just couldn't stand there and let him murder you,' Mrs Dora Wallace babbled. 'The man is most clearly deranged. No wonder, considering his tragic loss. I just knew he intended squeezing the life out of you.' At that Mrs Dora Wallace burst into tears. 'He's a monster,' she sobbed. 'An evil man. He deserved to die.'

'Well, I won't argue with you.' Miz Polly agreed.

'I must get home. I don't feel well. My heart...' Sobbing profusely Mrs Dora Wallace stumbled out of the laundry.

Miz Polly stared after her. 'What the hell is going on in this town?' she muttered to herself. She was damned if she knew!

Mrs Dora Wallace stumbled home. Poor Edward had declared his undying love for her and then she'd heard the rumours concerning Edward and Dotty Glover. In a fit of madness she'd paid two bums passing through town to tar and feather poor Edward, never dreaming the ordeal would kill him. And it was all on account of Theodore Black. She'd have to lie down. Her chest was hurting!

CHAPTER 12

Walter Thompson watched as the sealed coffins of the judge and two other men were loaded aboard the boxcar. The members of the hunting party who had given up the chase were already on board. He turned towards Nathaniel Standish. He cleared his throat. 'It might be better for you, Nathaniel, if you didn't return home just yet!'

'Why is that, Walter?'

'Well, your father isn't around to protect you. There's been rumours circulated, Nathaniel. Some of your so-called friends have been indiscreet. And so have you. There are certain among your father's friends who have heard the rumours.'

'So?' Nathaniel questioned arrogantly. 'The good name of Standish is already tarnished!'

'We are all agreed that Mrs Standish must have fallen prey to insanity. Her condition no way reflected upon the judge and yourself.'

Nathaniel shrugged. His expression was one of boredom. 'Where is this leading, Walter?' he enquired coolly.

Walter sighed. 'Your father voiced his suspicions concerning you, Nathaniel. We were friends, after all. We protected you, Nathaniel. False alibis were given. Good men lied for you. Why don't you stay here at least for a time.' He sighed. 'You have enough capital now to buy the late Theodore Black's ranch. Why don't you try your hand at becoming a gentleman rancher?' Nathaniel did not attempt to deny the unspoken allegations.

'Fortunately for you your victims were worthless, creatures of the gutter who had only themselves to blame, but even so they were attracting attention. There were too many, you see!' Walter Thompson climbed on board the eastward-bound train. Nathaniel, making no attempt to board the train, continued to stare as it began to pull away from the platform.

The idea of becoming a gentleman rancher was not without appeal. There would be plenty of business trips he would be required to make. It amused him to realize that he could with ease become a much-liked and respected man in Hawk's Head. And later, when the dust had settled, he would return East and take his place in society.

This town would suit him. A respectable rancher, a man of standing had been shot in the back by a woman, albeit a so-called respectable woman, and the events leading to the man's demise had been accepted at face value. The woman in question had given a statement to the lawman. And then shortly afterwards had suffered a heart attack and died. Whistling, he strolled back towards the hotel. Idly, he wondered how Cameron Hull was getting on.

Cameron Hull watched as Walter Thompson, Nathaniel and the others who lacked the stomach to see the hunt through to the end left for Hawk's Head. Hull decided that as a trophy he would take this Mr Noah's head. It could be carefully boiled, leaving just the bones of the skull and it could take pride of place in his display case. The man was a worthy opponent who had possessed the foresight to set a trap. He sighed. If only the judge had not charged into the shack like an enraged bull, good men would still be alive.

'The easier the kill, the less satisfaction there is,' he declared. 'We'll have them all eventually. They may well be foolish enough to believe we've called it a day. I'll take the lead. Keep your wits about you.'

The trail was easy to find. It wound upward, twisting and turning as it went, narrowing in places, widening in others. If he were fleeing for his life he would have left the goats behind but not these people. Despite the peril they were in they had refused to leave their livelihood behind. He understood that the Mexicans depended on the goats, but they were fools. Without the goats they might have stood a chance of losing themselves in this rocky terrain. He wondered whether Mr Noah intended to spring any more traps. If so, he would be ready.

Noah's main concern was making sure that nothing happened to Angelina. Her safety was paramount. He needed her. Without Angelina he'd never find his way out of this wilderness. He could not survive out here alone.

They were on foot. It was too dangerous to ride. To his surprise Mrs Standish was bearing up well. He glanced over his shoulder. As yet there was no sign of their pursuers but he knew it was too much to hope that the hunting party had given up the chase. For them it was a matter of life and death. To their pursuers this was sport!

'I do not like what you propose, Mr Noah.' Angelina broke the silence.

'I can't think of another way. It ain't much of a plan but I figure it will work. I want this over pretty damn quick. I've had a bellyful of this land. I ought never to have headed West. Yep! I left the city to avoid confrontation with the high and mighty Judge Elmore Standish and I've had nothing but trouble. So when this is over I'd be obliged if you'd get me back to Hawk's Head. I aim to deal with Theodore Black and whoever else gets in my way. And I ain't forgetting the galoots who put me from the train. But don't you worry, Miz

Angelina, I aim to keep you safe.'

'So I can guide you back to Hawk's Head?'

'I'd be obliged,' he rejoined.

'But Mr Noah, you are a fine man. I want you for myself. I have saved your life. You are in my debt.'

'Quit joshing, Miz Angelina,' he replied.

'Mr Noah, I do not like to think you only wish to keep me safe so that I can guide you back to Hawk's Head.'

'You're a fine woman, Miz Angelina.' He wondered where the hell this conversation was headed. 'Now, let's head for the bridge and hope we get there before we're overtaken.'

'Do you think they are following us, Mr Noah?'

'Yep. I guess there'll always be some that will not quit.'

The tracks left by their quarry led upwards. As the morning got under way it wasn't long before the sun hung a blazing ball of light in the sky and sweat drenched their clothing. Cameron Hull had decided that they must proceed on foot. Shale slipped beneath their feet. This trail was too damn dangerous to traverse other than on foot.

'A godforsaken place for godforsaken

people,' Cameron Hull observed as spirits flagged. He smiled at his companions. 'Gentlemen, this will be a hunting trip to remember. And I've a feeling the end is in sight.' He was the undisputed leader of the hunting party. His jaw tightened; they were all excellent shots. 'Just shoot them down when you see them,' he ordered.

'Even Mrs Standish?' The doctor amongst them was shocked.

'She may become a casualty,' Hull replied. 'But that cannot be helped. Our priority is to see this matter concluded speedily. We all have other concerns, lives to return to. So yes, when they are spotted take good aim, shoot to kill.' He paused. 'But I would be obliged if you would leave the head of the man Noah intact. I believe it belongs in my collection. The fellow has led us on a long chase. No doubt about that. He's been responsible for the deaths of fine men.'

There were murmurs of agreement. As he had guessed, they all wanted this over with quickly.

'Well, here it is!' Angelina pointed at the rope bridge. 'Across the other side, further down there's an old disused mine. Whoever owned it put up the bridge.' She turned to Noah.

'We can get across. I've done so before.'

Noah nodded.

'Just step on the bridge and don't look down,' she said. 'We must blindfold the horses and lead them across.'

He did not respond. He was feeling pretty damn sick. He balked at what had to be done. If it could be avoided he had no intention of shooting it out with the hunting party. He had no intention of even looking one of those varmints in the eye. Gritting his teeth he set off across the bridge. It seemed an eternity before they were all safely across.

'As soon as it is safe you come back for me,' he told Angelina.

She nodded. If he did not succeed, they were all dead. She did not think that they could outshoot the hunting party.

He watched them ride away. Oddly, it was not the thought of taking on the hunting party that made his stomach churn, it was being out here alone that unsettled him. And if they did not come back for him he knew he would never be able to find them out here. Tracking was not his forte. Serving drinks was what he knew. That and handling no-account drunks!

Patiently he set to work weakening the ropes that held the bridge; not too much, just enough to make it easier for when the time came. And when that was done, he lay down flat on sun-baked ground and pulled the cloth covering fashioned by Angelina over him. She'd done a good job, securing dried grasses and pieces of shrub on to the fabric. He lay at the edge of the bridge and waited, the razor-sharp blade Angelina had given him within easy grasp of his right hand, and a canteen of tepid water close by his left. He hoped the fine gentlemen in pursuit would show themselves pretty soon. But he was a patient man. Years of dealing with the troublemakers and fools who'd nightly crowded into Flannigan's bar had instilled a patience which had never been more needed than right now. Lives other than his own depended on him.

As they rounded a bend the rope bridge came into sight. It was the last thing they expected to see up here.

'Damn bastards!' Cameron Hull yelled, incensed by the sight.

'How the hell did they get across?' a companion asked.

'Maybe it's a trick. Maybe they haven't gone across.' There was a hopeful note in the speaker's voice which Hull quickly dispelled.

193

He studied the ground. 'No. They've gone across. I'd say they blindfolded the horses and got them across that way.'

'So we turn back.'

'And let two Mexicans, a scum of a bartender and the fool wife of Judge Standish outwit us?' Cameron Hull spat scornfully. 'If those carrion can get across this bridge then so can we.' He considered their position for a moment. 'They can't be far ahead. I'd say we should have them by nightfall.'

Across the bridge Noah lifted his head. He could see the hunters on the distant side. There seemed to be some sort of confrontation taking place. He guessed some of the party were not keen to tackle the bridge.

'It's settled. I'll take the lead.' Cameron Hull stepped on to the bridge. 'There's no way they can pick us off as we cross. There's no cover, nowhere for them to hide. If we keep our heads, this will be over by nightfall.'

It had to be now, Noah knew. They had almost reached the halfway point. He didn't yell to announce his presence, he didn't jump to his feet but came up on to his knees and slashed furiously at the weakened ropes.

Cameron Hull was the first to realize their danger. But there was little he could do. He released his horse and drew his pistol, but even as he fired he knew it was too late for all of them. His last thought as he fell was that he ought to have known that the bar-keeper would not fight fair.

Noah heard the screams. It was the horses he felt sorry for. He felt only anger and hatred for the men who had put him in this position. He raised his pistol and fired three times in rapid succession, signalling to Angelina that it was over.

While he waited for her he peered down into the gaping chasm below. He could see what remained of the hunting party far below, dead men and dead horses, their blood staining the rock-strewn floor. Merci-fully nothing moved. Far overhead, a speck against a clear blue sky, a buzzard circled. First there was one and then there were a whole lot more.

'You've saved us, Mr Noah,' Angelina declared. 'And when circumstances permit I aim to show my thanks in a way you won't forget.' She smiled. 'I'm hoping you won't be wanting to get back to Hawk's Head yet awhile, and if you do, all I can say is I'll get around to taking you back one day but that day ain't yet!'

Sometimes Miz Polly found herself wondering what had become of Noah. But she didn't spend much time wondering. She was pretty busy these days.

Her nose wrinkled as a stinking old galoot entered the laundry. 'Get these washed,' he grunted. He winked. 'I'll be over at the bath house cleaning myself up for the "ladies".'

She planted her hands on her hips. 'You can pay in advance. And as for the "ladies" – well, they have my sympathy.'

He laughed, showing yellowish teeth.

'Put the money down.' Hell, she wasn't going to take it from his hand.

'Are you afraid I can't pay, Miz Polly?'

'Pay up!' Miz Polly demanded, planting her hands on ample hips.

To her surprise he guffawed. 'A certain gent of your acquaintance told me that's what you would say.'

'What the hell are you talking about?'

He put the money to pay for his laundry carefully down on the table. 'Mr Noah sends his regards.'

'You've seen him!'

'Yep. He's alive and well.'

'Where the hell is he? Theodore Black is dead, some months back. Does he know?'

The old galoot laughed. 'Well, I don't

reckon Mr Noah is thinking about Theodore Black. He has other things on his mind. Anyway, he sends his regards and told me to give you this. Said to tell you to read it word for word.'

'What the hell!' She stared at the blood-stained leather-bound book.

'Seems this journal once belonged to a big shot named Cameron Hull. Mr Noah he said he ain't joshing. You're to read this journal, Miz Polly. He said maybe you need to know what's in it and maybe you don't. But you're to read it! Now when are my dudes going to be ready?'

'Get out of here, you old varmint.' Her voice had softened. 'Your dudes will be ready when they are ready. I'm overloaded with work. Fact is we're going to have to hire help.'

She put the journal carefully away. She'd read it by and by. The truth was she was rushed off her feet these days with Dotty's child to care for.

Pretending to be something he was not could be irksome at times but Nathaniel Standish had persevered. He owned the ranch belonging to the late Theodore Black but the ranch was managed in a vastly different way now. Farmers were treated with respect. If a widelooper was apprehended the thief was handed over to Sheriff Clem Sawyer. He attended Sunday service without fail and listened attentively as Pastor Webb ranted about the Hell that awaited those who did not repent. He nodded dutifully and hid his smile when the fool of a pastor welcomed Miz Polly, who had married Sheriff Sawyer, into the church. He himself had married Pastor Webb's sister Agnes.

He had only once almost committed an error of judgement. He had toyed with the idea of hiring the gunman Jericho to finish the job that his father's hunting party had failed to do.

'If anyone could have taken care of Mr Noah it would have been you, Jericho,' he had said jokingly.

'Hell, no,' the gunman had replied. 'Mrs Brannigan thinks highly of Mr Noah and I know better than to rile my sister.'

'You're a sensible man,' Nathaniel had said. 'A sensible man always knows who is in charge.' He turned away, aware that Jericho was eyeing him keenly, both men knowing that a question had been asked in a round-about way and answered in a roundabout way.

And now, as Nathaniel took tea with

Pastor Webb, he played the role of a meek husband to the hilt. 'If Mrs Standish wants to spend time back East then I know better than to argue. I've sent word to my lawyers to hire staff to get my former home ready and waiting. You've welcome to join us.'

'I feel I am needed here. Jericho is almost persuaded.'

'Almost persuaded?' Nathaniel raised a brow.

'He's been seeing this Anna, Miz Polly's partner at the laundry.' The pastor lowered his voice. 'I suspect misconduct.'

'And you've told him to steer clear of the laundry?'

'I am insisting he does right and marries the woman. If I leave now there is no one to act as his conscience.'

'I understand.' It was far better the fool of a pastor did not accompany them East. He could not wait to get back to his old haunts.

'Everything will have changed, Mr Noah,' Angelina said with conviction. They were waiting for the eastward-bound train, but not at Hawk's Head. It did not need to be said it was best to steer clear of that town. 'It has been four years, after all, Mr Noah.'

'But you're the one wanting to go back for

a visit.'

'I am curious to see what draws you to this place. And it is not as if you will be alone. I will be with you. I am looking forward to getting away from the goats.'

As the train drew into the station Mr Noah took his wife's arm and helped her into the rear carriage.

'Have you Mexicans got tickets?'

Noah raised his head. He remembered the voice and face. It was the conductor who'd drugged him and put him from the train to await Theodore Black.

'We have, friend.' Noah saw that the man did not remember him, perhaps because of the clothes and beard. Cold blue eyes from a sun-tanned face stared at the conductor.

'Just asking, sir.' The conductor backed away, sensing this would be a dangerous passenger to rile.

'That's him?' Angelina asked, noticing Noah's change of expression.

He nodded. 'I do believe that when we reach our destination this train will be missing a conductor.'

Nathaniel Standish settled back against the upholstery of the first-class carriage. 'There will be a carriage at your disposal at all times, Mrs Standish. And it will be my pleasure to introduce your to the dressmakers my late mother patronized.'

Agatha Standish smiled. Nathaniel was the perfect husband. She would not be so indiscreet as to point out that they could not be sure his mother was indeed deceased. She wondered how she could have ever imagined herself drawn to a ruffian such as Mr Noah when a fine gentleman such as Nathaniel had been just around the corner. She would be forever grateful to Nathaniel's mother. If the woman had not become insane and run away to the West she would never have met Nathaniel.

As Noah stood outside the station with his wife, surrounded by hustle and bustle, carriages and people, voices calling loudly, it hit him hard that he did not, after all, want to be here. He preferred the solitude of the hills, and the clean air of the wilderness. He hadn't realized how much he had changed.

'Well, Mrs Noah, we'll find a rooming-house and settle in.'

Nathaniel Standish saw his wife settled into the four-poster bed which had once been used by his mother. A sleeping-draught slipped into her hot milk saw her go out as though she had been poleaxed. Nathaniel slipped out into the night and headed for the worst part of town.

Women in their tawdry finery were still around as he remembered, still desperate for custom, and he found one without difficulty. He was going to make the most of his time here. He had a nose for trouble. He would know when it was time to leave. That would be before questions were asked!

Dotty Glover sat in a restaurant in the best part of town. With her was her gentleman protector, a rotund man in an expensive suit. He was the owner of the restaurant, among other less respectable concerns.

To the man's astonishment a smile appeared on Dotty's face. 'It's Mr Noah!' she exclaimed. 'Look!' She pointed. 'Send a waiter to invite them to join us for tea?'

'But...'

'I wouldn't be here if it were not for Mr Noah and his meddling.'

Her companion clicked his fingers and sent a waiter scurrying out.

'Seems Mr Noah isn't keen to come in,' the man observed, noticing how the large woman beside Mr Noah was obliged to take his arm and steer him into the restaurant.

'Miss Dotty, you're looking well,' Noah remarked as he sat down. 'Let me introduce you to Mrs Noah.'

'But Mr Noah, what's happened to you? Why, as I recall you were smartly dressed.'

'Say, are you the Mr Noah who used to work at Flannigan's?'

Mr Noah nodded. 'Those days are gone. If you are thinking of offering me a job I am obliged to refuse. Mrs Noah and myself have seen enough of the city. We're headed home.'

'You know who I am?'

'I've seen a few familiar faces. I know who you are. Folk seem wary of mentioning your name, Mr Warrington. I guess you're running the East Side now!'

Warrington nodded. 'I have an interest in most things around here.' He glanced keenly at Noah. 'Three of the street girls have gone missing. You haven't heard anything? One was fished out of the river in a bad way.'

'Missing a finger?' Noah asked.

'What do you knew about that?'

'Not a damn thing. Although according to the journal of a certain Cameron Hull, Nathaniel Standish was suspected of certain matters. Hull believed Nathaniel had made himself a necklace out of the finger-bones.'

Noah shook his head. 'But last I heard Standish was ranching in Hawk's Head. Folk seem to have accepted him. I don't go to town much these days, and I steer clear of Hawk's Head. Fact is, I've had my fill of trouble and killing. I prefer goats to people. Thank you kindly for the tea, Miss Dotty. You take care now. We'll be on our way. We've a train to catch.'

'Poor Mr Noah. What's happened to him? Why, folks were scared of him,' Dotty said to Warrington. 'He gunned down my worthless kin without batting an eye and now all he wants is to get back to his goats. It's Mrs Noah. She's ruined him.' But her companion wasn't listening. Warrington happened to know that Nathaniel Standish was back in town.

Nathaniel sighed. In a few days' time he would be returning to Hawk's Head. He knew he was pushing his luck, which had been good so far, but he could not resist one last kill. As Agatha slept he slipped out of the house. The road outside the large Standish house was deserted now except for a waiting coachman. Nathaniel hesitated. He'd noticed the East Side had changed. One man, he'd heard, was running the criminal element that infested the streets. Snatching women from the street was more risky than it had been four years ago. He shook his head, quickening his stride eager anticipation.

The blow that felled him came from behind. It caught him by surprise. He'd had no inkling that anyone was behind him. Half-unconscious he nevertheless realized that he was being bundled into the waiting carriage.

Waiting in his slaughterhouse Warrington reflected that perhaps it was just as well that Mr Noah wasn't staying around. He'd sensed the man could be a dangerous opponent.

'If Mr Noah were here I would not pay you a dime,' old Flannigan had griped as he had paid his protection money. Flannigan's nephew, newly arrived from Ireland, ran the bar now.

Dotty was wrong. Mr Noah was still a dangerous man. He was a dangerous man himself and recognized another when he encountered one. But the difference was that Mr Noah was an honest man, while he himself was crooked through and through. The door opened and two of his men came in. They had Nathaniel Standish.

'Take his shirt off,' Warrington ordered, wanting to see if Standish was wearing the necklace.

It was there, as he had thought it would be: a necklace of finger-bones threaded on a string of leather. Coldly he eyed Standish. The man was handsome. And rich. Two attributes that would have made Warrington dislike him without even knowing what Standish was capable of.

'I'll have to make an example of you,' he told Standish. 'You see, those women paid me to work on my streets, not much, it is true, but thanks to you word has spread that I can't keep my streets safe for those I let work them. Nobody gets killed on my streets without my say-so. And you, you come back from your fancy ranch where you ought to have stayed and go on a killing spree.'

'I'll pay you,' Nathaniel gabbled. 'You can't pretend you cared about those no-goods.'

'I won't pretend. But they paid for the right to be on my streets, it being understood that they would be kept safe. My reputation is at stake. Scream all you like, Mr Standish, no one will hear you in my slaughterhouse.' He smiled. 'Mr Noah would most likely make it quick for you, but then I'm not Mr Noah.'

The publishers hope that this book has given you enjoyable reading. Large Print Books are especially designed to be as easy to see and hold as possible. If you wish a complete list of our books please ask at your local library or write directly to:

Dales Large Print Books
Magna House, Long Preston,
Skipton, North Yorkshire.
BD23 4ND

This Large Print Book, for people
who cannot read normal print,
is published under the auspices of

THE ULVERSCROFT FOUNDATION